# *The Mysterious* — 
# Traveling Trunk

## Linda C. Land

Order this book online at www.trafford.com
or email orders@trafford.com

Most Trafford titles are also available at major online book retailers.

Printed in the United States of America.

ISBN: 978-1-4269-6161-8 (sc)
ISBN: 978-1-4269-6160-1 (hc)
ISBN: 978-1-4269-6159-5 (e)

Library of Congress Control Number: 2011904676

*Trafford rev.04/07/2011*

 www.trafford.com

**North America & International**
toll-free: 1 888 232 4444 (USA & Canada)
phone: 250 383 6864 ✦ fax: 812 355 4082

Dedication
For Tosha and Patty

# Preface

I wrote this story for my two oldest granddaughters, Tosha and Patty. They have always loved spooky stories, so in 1999 I wrote one especially for them. At the time, Tosha was ten years old, and Patty was nine. This story is full of their individual personalities and passion for adventure. Their love of this story motivated me to continue writing children's chapter books.

# Acknowledgments

A huge thank you to my busy daughter Michelle, whose on-line communicating, editing, and re-writing is a large part of making my stories a finished product. I want to give a big thank you to my friend Julie who took over the job of all the initial edits. Thanks for all your hard work. I also want to thank Tosha and Patty who are now college students. Thanks for taking part in the editing process. I couldn't do it without you.

# CHAPTER ONE

# THE SECRET

Finally, they were on their way to Patty's house. Tosha was looking forward to spending the night at her cousin's. Tosha was a bright ten-year-old, with a fair complexion that tanned easily in the summer. She had beautiful strawberry-blond hair, blue-green eyes, and just a hint of freckles scattered across her nose. She was a leader by nature, always eager to learn and was interested in everything.

She could hardly wait to show her cousin the old mansion she had discovered. The last time Tosha's mom had driven her home from Patty's house, they had gone a different way and Tosha noticed a big, old vacant house just a couple of blocks from her cousin's. Shrubs and bushes had gone unattended for many years and were large and shaggy. All this growth blocked much of Tosha's view of the interesting house. It sat far back off the road and was surrounded by a high, iron fence. Tosha's mind filled with wonder about the place. It was so mysterious looking. This place was just the sort of thing that her cousin would love. They both enjoyed telling scary stories and reading mysteries. She was certain Patty would agree that this old mansion was fascinating.

Tosha's daydreaming was interrupted when her mom pulled their car into her cousin's driveway. She looked up, and saw Patty running out of the house to greet her. Tosha threw open the car door and jumped out, grabbing her overnight bag and backpack.

The two girls ran to each other. Standing side by side, one would think they were the same age. There was very little difference between their height and their overall size, even though Tosha was eighteen months older and one grade ahead of Patty in school.

Patty had large brown eyes always full of expression, and light brown hair. She had a dark complexion, and always looked like she had a tan, even in the winter. She was a happy kid, full of energy and natural curiosity. Patty was far more cautious than Tosha, preferring to think first and act later. Both girls loved adventure, being outside, reading books, and listening to their newest CD's.

Tosha said her goodbyes to her mom, grabbed Patty by the hand, and headed for her cousin's bedroom. She was very excited about the mansion and couldn't wait to show it to her cousin. As they ran into the house and down the hall, they failed to notice Patty's five year old little sister, Lori Lynn, who was right on their heels. When they abruptly shut the bedroom door behind them, they heard her cry of protest. The cousins stood silently at the door, expecting to hear from Patty's mom.

Patty frowned and rolled her brown eyes toward the door. "She follows me everywhere. You're lucky Amber is too little to be in your way all the time," she complained in a low whisper.

The girls remained at the door for a few more seconds, but when no scolding words were heard, they figured they were okay for now. Lori Lynn must have decided to find something else to do. Patty's mom was really good about understanding that the older girls needed to have their own space once in a while.

Tosha dropped her bags on the floor and shot Patty a mysterious gaze. "What?" Patty questioned. "Why are you looking at me like that?"

Tosha could hardly contain herself. "Oh Patty, I have something I want to show you. It's so cool, and it's only a few blocks from your house. I'm not going to tell you what it is, I want to surprise you. You're going to love it, but we have to figure out how we can get away from the house for awhile." The suspenseful expression covering her cousin's face sparked Patty's curiosity.

"I don't know," her cousin responded, trying to think of an idea. "I guess we could tell mom we want to go down the street and play with Angelica."

With that, Tosha's plan was put into action. Patty asked her mom if it was okay that they go down the street and play at Angelica's house for a while. Patty's mom agreed, and gave them two hours to play before they needed to be home. Patty was a little worried about lying to her mom. She was not in the habit of doing that sort of thing, and she knew it was wrong. But, Tosha had said it was something really cool and that Patty would love it. One little white lie seemed harmless enough.

With backpacks slung over their shoulders, the two girls were on their way, down the street to the corner then right two blocks. Tosha was so excited! She just couldn't wait to see Patty's expression when she saw the mansion for the first time. This would be the biggest adventure of their lives. Tosha imagined exploring the old house. It would be more fun than the haunted houses they had gone through last Halloween. She remembered back to the day she had seen it for the first time. She had asked her mom about it. Her mother told her that a rich family had owned the mansion many years ago. The mansion had been empty for years, but not long ago it had been purchased by a women's group who planned to restore it and turn it into a museum or something. Tosha was so lost in her own thoughts that she hardly heard the questions her cousin was asking her.

"What could be so interesting around here?" Patty drilled her cousin with questions. "How far is it? Why can't you tell me now? Why does it have to be a surprise?" Her cousin asked one question after another.

Tosha turned her attention to Patty. "Boy, your dad was right when he teased you the other day about all the questions you ask. Remember what he said to you, 'Why Patty...why... why Patty, why?'" Tosha smiled over her shoulder at Patty, and was rewarded by a big smile from her.

"Yeah, he loves to say that to me every time I ask him something," Patty replied.

It was a beautiful May afternoon with the promise of great springtime weather. All the flowers were blooming, and their delicious scents floated in the air. The girls did not notice though, they had other things on their minds.

As they walked along Tosha realized that school would be out in a couple of weeks, and they would have the whole summer ahead of them. There would be plenty of time to explore the old mansion, and that was exactly what she had in mind. She thought it would be so neat to go all through that big house. She wondered what sort of intriguing things they might find inside it.

It took only fifteen minutes to get to their destination. As they approached the overgrown area, Tosha stopped and gazed at the dark structure looming over the tops of the trees. Then she turned to look at her cousin and said, "Patty, I present you with your surprise. This is better than any book or any story you have ever enjoyed." Tosha watched her cousin's expression with eager anticipation.

Patty slowly walked over to the tall iron fence. Holding onto the bars, she peered between them. She could hardly believe her eyes. Patty had lived in this neighborhood for nine years, all of her life, but she had never noticed this place before today. The huge house was built out of dark gray stone. The windows were tall and narrow, and had a forbidding appearance to them, gloomy and gray. There were bars on all the windows, making the house look more like a prison. Oh my, Patty thought. Even the roof, which was tall and pointed with high peaks, seemed to be the same dead gray color. The entire house had a bleak, abandoned look about it. Green moss clung to the stone walls, adding to the eerie look of the structure.

Patty stepped back from the fence. Tosha was at her side trying to read the mixture of expressions that crossed her face. Patty's big brown eyes were now even larger as she stared ahead of her. Neither girl realized that they were holding hands, and without meaning to, Patty was squeezing Tosha's unmercifully. This caused Tosha to scream in pain which immediately broke the trance Patty was in. As they looked at each other, the unspoken words were in both of their eyes. *Now* what do we do?

Patty knew exactly what she wanted to do. Without saying a word, she grabbed Tosha by her arm and started pulling her back towards the street. She'd decided she wanted no part of this big surprise her cousin had for her. No matter what Tosha had in mind, Patty was certain she wanted nothing to do with it.

"Wait Patty, where are we going? We just got here." Tosha protested, while at the same time tried unsuccessfully to pull her arm free from her cousin's tight grip.

Patty stopped abruptly and looked Tosha square in the face. Tosha could see the panic in her cousin's eyes as Patty said, "That is the scariest place I've ever seen in my life. Why did you bring me here? No, don't answer that. I think I know exactly what you have in mind, and you can count me out! I'm going straight home and telling my mom I want to move. I can't believe I live so close to such a spooky place!" Patty paused and stubbornly crossed her arms over her chest.

Tosha couldn't believe her ears. "What are you afraid of? It's just an old house. It's not like it is haunted or anything," Tosha said in an exasperated tone. She had been so sure that once her cousin saw this amazing place, she would be as eager to explore it as Tosha was.

Patty rolled her eyes doubtfully. "What makes you so sure, who made you the expert on it?"

In defense, Tosha told Patty about the conversation she'd had with her dad on the subject. "I asked my dad just last week if there really are such things as ghosts. He said, 'No, things like that don't exist in real life, only in movies and books,' and I believe him."

Of the two girls, Tosha was the risk taker. Patty was more cautious, which made them a good team. Where many times Tosha would rush into things, Patty would caution her cousin, and therefore slow her down a bit. Patty was certain that this was one of those...*take it slow*...times.

Tosha had to find a way to convince Patty not to go home yet. "Okay Patty, I know it looks scary, but let's not go back yet. Give me a chance to prove to you that the house is not as spooky as it looks. I've been dying to get a closer look at this mansion ever since I saw it. I wanted this to be something you and I would do together. Now you want to spoil everything." Tosha could usually get Patty to see things her way. This time she was trying to make her feel guilty, but was it working? She couldn't tell yet. All she could do was hope.

Patty looked down at the ground, kicking at a pebble with the toe of her shoe as she thought about what Tosha had said. Finally she looked up and replied, "Okay, we will just look, and then we'll go home. Promise me?"

"Okay," Tosha said, and immediately started pulling Patty back to the big iron fence. "Come on, we're wasting time!"

Tosha's plan was to find a way through the fence, and once they got through the fence, she hoped to find a way into the mansion. Surely, once they got closer to the house, Patty would want to go inside as much as she did. Tosha couldn't explain why she was so fascinated by this place. She was bursting with curiosity about the mansion and the family who had built it. She had questioned her mom that day in the car, asking her about the family who had lived there. "What were their names? Did they have kids? How long did they live there? How many years has the house been empty?"

Tosha's mom had laughed, "Well, so many questions." She had smiled at her daughter and said, "If you're really that interested, we can go to the library and see what information they have on it, there should be something on file." Tosha was delighted. Her mom was so good about taking time with her, whether it was a school project or just something Tosha was interested in, and this big old house interested her very much. Her mother had promised her they would go to the library as soon as school was out.

As Patty and Tosha worked their way through the bushes around the fence, a different part of the house came into view. There was a terrace on the upper level of the second story. It looked as though the house had at least three levels, and probably an attic. Tosha had never been in an attic, but she was sure that if there was anything left in the house of any interest, that's where it would be.

Patty was not thrilled about crawling through so much shrubbery. She hated bugs and worried that they might get in her hair, so most of her attention was focused on the bushes, inspecting them every step of the way. When Tosha abruptly stopped, Patty plowed into her with enough force to knock her off her feet and to the ground. This jolt, while a surprise, did not sway Tosha's intent gaze at the house. Patty's eyes followed Tosha's.

They were now looking at what must be the back of the house. It was incredible! There were several large fountains located in the center of a huge patio. A short stone wall surrounded the entire area. The windows visible on this side of the house were the same style as those on the front of the house. There were dozens of them, however Patty noticed that these windows did not have iron bars on them. From back here, the house seemed nicer, warmer, almost inviting. The whole appearance seemed different for some reason. This helped Patty to relax. She couldn't believe the transformation that had taken place. Maybe it was the beautiful patio. It made it seem more like a house that someone had once lived in and loved.

Until now, the girls had both been pretty quiet. Patty broke the silence, and shared with Tosha the change she noticed in the house. "It doesn't seem so scary anymore. I wonder why?"

Tosha was very relieved to hear her cousin's change of heart. She quickly took advantage of the moment. "Patty, we've got to get closer."

Patty's head spun around. She stared at her cousin. Cautiously, Patty asked the dreaded question, "What exactly do you mean by *closer?*"

"Well, I want to get through this fence. We can't see anything from way back here. Don't you want to, too?" Tosha urged, hopeful that Patty would agree.

"Hold on Tosha! You said we were just going to look at the house from the fence, and then go home. Don't think that just because I said the place looked less scary, that I want to move in. Besides, we've already been gone too long, and if my mom calls Angelica's house, we're both in big trouble!"

Tosha was ready for this reaction. She glanced at her watch and with a smile on her face, she quickly replied, "Patty, it won't take long to look around the house. Your mom gave us two hours and we've only been gone about twenty minutes. I didn't say we would stay outside the fence, I said I wanted to get a closer look. This is not close, way back here. We have plenty of time." Tosha watched her cousin think about everything she had said. Then Tosha had an idea. "Patty, I dare you! I double-dare you!" She challenged her cousin. Tosha just couldn't help herself. She wanted to get inside that house, and she didn't want to do it alone.

Patty stiffened up and then started to squirm around a bit. Instantly, Tosha felt guilty about daring her cousin. She reached out and put her hand on her cousin's shoulder. "Oh, come on Patty. You're always reading all those mystery books, can't you see the mystery in this house? Wouldn't you like to be a part of an adventure, instead of only reading about them?"

Patty frowned and looked at her cousin. With her head slightly tilted to one side, she said, "Doing something like trespassing isn't an adventure, it's more like breaking the law. Also, reading a scary book and doing something scary, is not the same thing. What exactly is it you're looking for Tosha? We could get into so much trouble doing this."

Tosha shrugged her shoulders, "I'm not really looking for anything. I just think it would be so cool to go through an old place like this. I thought you would think so too, but I guess I was wrong. I don't plan on causing any harm to anything, I would never do that. It's just interesting looking, it's so old. It would be like walking through a history book." Tosha's curious smile had turned into a frown. Her eyes filled with disappointment, and her shoulders slumped forward.

Now it was Patty's turn to feel guilty. She didn't want to be a drag. "Okay," she said, "but we will be grounded for life if my parents find out about this. You lead the way. I will follow, but let's stay close together."

Tosha was thrilled. Her face once again glowed with excitement as they resumed their struggle along the fence. After a few more minutes, they came to a place where a large dead tree had fallen over on the fence. It had bent the bars just enough for two small girls to climb through. "What a break!" Tosha exclaimed. She was certain it was a sign, a good sign. She just knew they were meant to find this place and explore it.

Tosha was so excited she could hardly control herself. She turned to Patty and said, "Just look here Patty. This is too good to be true. It's as if we were supposed to find this spot. Can you believe it? This is just too cool!"

Patty turned her head so Tosha couldn't see her face. She was too scared to share her cousin's enthusiasm. She rolled her eyes toward heaven, and silently prayed nothing bad would happen to them. She had such an uneasy feeling about all this.

The two girls walked across the lawn and onto the patio. They were once again holding hands. Patty couldn't believe she had allowed Tosha to talk her into this. She just knew it was all going to end badly; if not here at this awful house, then surely at home when her mom discovered what they'd been up to. Oh gosh, thought Patty, Mom and Dad just can't find out. They will never let me out of my room again for the rest of my life. I'm sure of it. Patty was consumed with guilt.

While Patty was thinking troubled thoughts, Tosha's mind raced ahead. She knew her cousin was unnerved about this amazing old mansion, but she was hopeful that once they got inside, Patty would find it as interesting as Tosha knew it would be. Using her most convincing tone, Tosha said, "Gosh, I wonder how many rooms this old place has. Do you suppose there's anything inside, like old pictures or maybe some of those old fashioned hats they used to wear? Let's see if we can find an unlocked door or window so we can take a look inside."

Patty allowed her eyes to roam over the back part of the house where they were standing. It was so big and ancient looking, overgrown with vines and weeds. She briefly wondered how long it had been vacant. What if there was such a thing as ghosts? What if some raggedy homeless person was living inside? Her imagination envisioned all sorts of shadowy figures looming inside those cold gray walls. No, she wanted no part of it. She put her hands on her hips. "Who cares if there is old stuff in there? I sure don't, and even if there is, then what? I think we should go home and forget all about this place."

Tosha wasn't giving up, she was determined to explore it even if she had to do it alone. Patty was too much of a worrier, and was being too cautious. After all, they weren't going to hurt anything, she just wanted to look around a little. With a glance at her watch, Tosha said to her cousin, "Patty, we still have over an hour before we have to be home, and we're wasting time. I'm going to walk the rest of the way around the house. I want to see if there is a way in. If you won't come with me, then I'll go the rest of the way by myself. You wait right here. I'll be back in a few minutes, okay?"

Patty realized that Tosha was not going to give up, so she thought about her options. She could leave now and go home alone, or she could go around the house and help Tosha search, or she could take Tosha's suggestion and wait here on the somewhat pleasant patio. She knew if she went with her cousin and they did find a way into the house, Tosha would insist that Patty explore the house with her, but Patty absolutely did not want to go inside. After a moment, she reluctantly agreed to wait on the patio. The minute she shook her head up and down in a wordless okay, Tosha took flight and ran off around the house, checking every window and door along the way. Climbing through many more bushes, she was filled with high hopes of finding a way into the alluring structure.

Once alone, standing so near the cold grayness of the big house, Patty regretted her decision. She hated the idea of being so close to the creepy house without Tosha at her side. Standing there with her head down, she noticed something engraved on the surface of the patio. She bent down to inspect the inscription closer. Patty saw two tiny footprints, and just below them were three words. 'OUR SWEET EMILY'

Absentmindedly, Patty lowered her fingers and gently caressed the small imprints. Slowly, she stood up and moved from where she was standing. She walked over towards the windows that lined the back of the house. Patty wondered, who was Emily? How many years ago had those tiny imprints been made? Did she once live here, and play on this very patio? She leaned forward and peeked in through the windows. It was so dark inside the house she couldn't really make out much. Leaning her head against the glass, she thought it was just as well. She closed her eyes and told herself she wasn't interested in seeing the inside anyway. As she stood there, with her back to the patio, she thought of what she would say to Tosha the minute she came back. She was prepared to tell her cousin that she was going home, with or without her. Exploring this old place just wasn't something she wanted to do. *Sure*, Patty was the tiniest bit curious. Anyone would be, but it was dark and scary-looking on the outside, the inside could only be worse.

Patty's head was still resting against one of the patio windows. She was so deep in thought she didn't notice the movement in the bushes beside her. A sudden noise startled her and she whirled around, her eyes focusing in its direction. She couldn't believe what she saw. Her mind quickly responded to the vision before her, she screamed! Her only thought now, was one of escape.

Patty jumped back so hard and so fast that the window she had been leaning against earlier, now swung open and she fell backwards. Momentarily dazed, she found herself flat on her back, on the floor inside the house. The force of the fall had knocked the wind out of her. While she struggled hard to catch her breath, the little skunk that had come from its hiding place in the bushes, quickly disappeared back into them. It took a minute for the pain to subside before she could sit up. As she got her bearings and looked around, she noticed the window she had fallen through was not a window at all. It was a door, and had easily given way to the sudden force put upon it. Patty jumped to her feet, and moved rapidly in a forward motion, straight out the door. She headed across the patio, her eyes searching for the opening in the fence, where she knew she would find freedom from this place. In her haste, she failed to notice that she had dropped her backpack. It was lying on the floor where she had fallen.

Meanwhile, Tosha was working her way to every window and door she could reach, trying desperately to find one that would open. She had almost run out of possibilities when she heard Patty scream. Never, in all her life, had she heard a more terrified scream. Tosha immediately gave up her search for entry and took off running in the direction of the patio, as fast as her legs would carry her.

Tosha rounded the corner of the patio at the exact moment Patty was coming out at full speed. The two girls collided unexpectedly, both screaming in shock and pain as they fell to the ground. Unharmed, but both confused and alarmed, they scrambled to their feet and without a word to each other, ran to the fallen tree and squeezed through to the other side of the fence.

Through the fence and up the street they ran, covering at least a block before their pace slowed. They both struggled to catch their breath. They looked at each other, and at the same time started talking, their questions and explanations blending together in total confusion.

Patty was half-screaming and half-crying. She was trying to tell Tosha what happened with the skunk, and how she actually found herself inside the house. Tosha was shouting out questions regarding Patty's screaming and why she was running. Abruptly, Tosha stopped talking. She straightened up, looked Patty directly in the eyes and asked, "What did you say? Did I hear you right? *You* were *in* the *house?*"

Patty quickly responded by nodding her head up and down. "Yes, yes I was in the house!" she exclaimed.

Tosha could hardly believe her ears. "How did you manage that?" she asked, confused.

Patty's brown eyes were full of excitement. "I *fell* in, that's what I've been trying to tell you." Patty continued her explanation of what had happened.

Tosha visualized the whole scene in her mind. When Patty got to the part about the skunk, Tosha started laughing.

She couldn't help herself. She laughed so hard that she fell to the ground doubled over in pain.

Patty stopped the description of the skunk episode in mid-sentence. Her face was turning red, and her arms were tightly folded across her chest in anger. She was clearly not happy with Tosha's reaction to her close encounter. She would have appreciated a little understanding. She stood there looking down at Tosha, waiting for her cousin to regain control of herself. Patty had a thing or two she wanted to say to her, but Tosha's laughter was too contagious. Patty suddenly found herself letting go of her anger as she joined Tosha and also started giggling uncontrollably. She had to admit it was pretty funny, but it would have been a lot funnier if the skunk had found Tosha instead of her.

As they rolled around in the grass giggling, Patty spoke her thoughts out loud. "Boy, I sure am happy to be away from that place. Tosha, if there are skunks living in the bushes around the patio, I'll bet there are all sorts of awful things living inside that house. I don't want to ever come back here, okay?"

"Patty, I understand how you feel. Really I do! I bet you would enjoy inspecting the inside of the house though. It's got to be nicer inside than it is outside. Let's not talk about it right now. I have an idea." Tosha looked at her watch. "We have about forty- five minutes left. Let's go by Angelica's house. After all, that's where we're supposed to be. Would that make you feel better?"

Patty thought about that for a moment, and she decided she liked this idea. Patty had been feeling guilty about lying to her mom. This would almost make things right. "Yes, that's a great idea, let's go."

Tosha didn't want to argue anymore with Patty about the mansion, but she couldn't wait to go back, especially now that she knew how to get in. She sat up, shaking her head thinking about how she had worked so hard crawling around the house through all those awful bushes, trying to find a way in, and Patty, who didn't want to go near the place, fell in without even trying. Wouldn't you know it!

Tosha stood up and reached over for her backpack. Patty turned to do the same and was shocked to realize her backpack was not there. Patty asked Tosha in a panicked voice, "Where is my backpack? Do you see it anywhere?"

Tosha looked around her, "No Patty, I don't see it. Where do you remember having it last?"

Patty's hands flew to her mouth. Her tone was one of total despair. "Oh my gosh, I must have dropped it in the house when I fell. That must be where it is." Patty was clearly upset. Everything important to her was in her backpack, but there was no way she would go back for it now, no way. "Come on," Patty said flatly, "we'd better get going to Angelica's house. We'll worry about my backpack later."

Tosha didn't even suggest going back to the house right then. She knew Patty wasn't up to it, but it did give her an idea. She knew they would have to go back for the backpack eventually. She would just wait. As they walked to Angelica's house, they promised each other that today's events would be their secret. They would never tell anyone about the old mansion.

CHAPTER TWO

# GRAYBROOK

Two weeks later

School was out, and today Tosha and her mom were going to the library. She had been counting down the days. Her mom made arrangements to take Amber to their Grandma's house so it would be just Tosha and her mom. After all, the library was no place for a busy one-year-old.

Once at the library, Tosha and her mother found all kinds of information on the mansion. It even had a name, which Tosha thought suited. The house was called Graybrook. It was built in 1899 by the Wareham family. The family lived in the mansion from 1899 to 1939. Most of the information the library had was about the house itself, but Tosha wanted to learn more about the Wareham family. Unfortunately, there weren't many details available on the family. The librarian told Tosha's mom that the Women's League, who now owned the house, had a lot of information on the family who had built it. Tosha's mom got the address, and promised her daughter she would write them.

Three days later, Tosha was in her room reading a book. It had been raining for two days, and she was getting a bad case of cabin fever. Her mom came into her room with terrific news.

"Tosha, how would you like to spend a week at Patty's house? In a couple days I have to go out of town for the agency."

Her mom had gone back to work part-time for the travel agency she worked for before Amber was born. She sometimes went out of town for a day or two, but never a whole week. This was just the break Tosha had been waiting for.

She looked up at her mom in disbelief. She had just been thinking about Patty and Graybrook, which was on her mind all the time. Tosha jumped off her bed so fast that all her books scattered every which way. She hugged her mom and ran to the phone to call Patty.

Ten minutes later Tosha and Patty were on the phone making plans for her visit, but nothing was said about the mansion. Tosha knew they shouldn't discuss it over the phone, and she wanted to wait for the right moment to bring it up. The wheels were turning in Tosha's head, and Patty knew it.

It was late afternoon the following day, when Tosha and her mom headed for Patty's house. She sat quietly looking out the car window, deep in thought. She was hoping that Patty would be willing to go back to Graybrook by now. She was certain her cousin would be.

When she arrived at Patty's it was dinnertime. When they finished eating, the two girls went to Patty's room. Since it was too wet to play outside, they decided to make a tent over the bunk-beds using some old sheets. Patty's little sister, Lori Lynn, was right there wanting to help. The three girls worked on the tent for about an hour, until they had everything just right. They spread out their sleeping bags and pulled all the pillows off the bed and placed them inside the make-shift tent. They were going to sleep in it and pretend they were camping out. They started getting ready for bed.

Lori Lynn ran to her room to put on her pajamas. She wanted to sleep with the big girls tonight. Tosha grabbed her backpack and sat it right next to her pillow. She made herself comfortable and pulled her flashlight and book out of her backpack. She expected Patty to join her, but instead Patty stood at the foot of her sleeping bag looking over at her cousin. Tosha looked up at her, "What are you waiting for? I know you must have a good book you're reading, you always do."

Patty glanced over her shoulder to make sure her little sister wasn't coming back yet. She plopped down onto her sleeping bag. Looking with envy at Tosha's book, Patty confessed. "I have a big problem, and I hesitate to even tell you because I know my problem is going to make you happy!"

Confused, Tosha tilted her head and frowned at her cousin. "What are you talking about? What makes you think that *you* having a big problem would make *me* happy?"

"Well, it's my library book. It's due to be turned in to the library in four days. My big problem is that I don't have the book."

"What, you lost the book you checked out of the county library? Do you know you'll have to pay for it, or should I say your parents will have to pay for it? How did you manage to lose a library book?" Tosha couldn't believe her cousin had been so careless. "Wait a minute! Why do you think something awful like this would make me happy?"

Patty moved closer to Tosha and once again glanced over her shoulder. Lori still hadn't returned to join them. Patty lowered her voice to a whisper, "My library book is in my backpack." Her face was consumed with worry.

Tosha really tried to hide her obvious joy, but she did not succeed.

Patty quickly read the delighted expression on her cousin's face. She struggled to keep her voice down. "See, I told you it would make you happy." Patty threw herself face down into her pillow. She was angry with herself for being so careless as to have left her backpack at that awful, gloomy old mansion.

Tosha instantly regretted allowing her joy to show. "Patty, I'm sorry, really I am! If the idea of going back bothers you that much, I will go there by myself and get your backpack for you. After all, it wasn't your fault that you left it there. You were frightened. If it was anyone's fault, it was mine. I was the one that wanted you to go there with me!" Tosha had never seen her cousin so upset.

Before Patty had a chance to respond, Lori Lynn came back into the room, her favorite stuffed animal and blanket in tow.

When they were settled in for the night, Tosha suggested they tell each other scary stories. This was usually one of Patty and Tosha's favorite sleepover traditions, so they thought this was a great idea, however, Lori Lynn did not share their enthusiasm. She hated scary stories, so she decided to leave the room to find a friendlier place in the house.

Once she was gone, the girls had the privacy they needed. Patty and Tosha both started talking at the same time. Then Patty placed her fingers over her cousin's lips to silence her. "Tosha, let me say this before I change my mind. I will go back there with you. I would never expect you to go to the mansion all by yourself. We'll go back together. I knew you would want to go back. Maybe this is a sign, a good one I hope."

Tosha rolled over and gazed at Patty with one eyebrow raised. She had a mysterious look on her face, as if she had a secret she wasn't sure she wanted to share.

Patty looked at her cousin with interest. "What are you thinking Tosha? You have that look in your eyes. Tell me what you're up to."

Both girls sat up in their little tent area almost nose to nose, with only a flashlight on. Tosha started telling Patty about what she had learned about Graybrook. "Patty, just think, it was built in 1899 so it's over one-hundred years old. Isn't that cool?"

Patty listened as her cousin shared everything she had discovered about the mansion at the library, all the cool stuff she had discovered about the house and the family. Patty's eyes began to show some interest. She loved the idea of the house having a name, and was amazed by how old it was. She wanted to know more about the people who had lived there and what happened to them. Suddenly, Patty remembered what she had seen on the patio that day. "Oh Tosha, I just remembered something. When we were at the…I mean at Graybrook I saw something."

"What was it, what did you see?" Tosha asked impatiently.

"On the patio, there was an impression of a baby's footprints. You know, like the ones in our baby books, except this one was in cement. Just below them, there was an inscription that read…*OUR SWEET EMILY.*" Tosha's face lit up with interest, "Wow Patty that is so cool! Is that all it said? Was there a date or anything else?"

"No," Patty said shaking her head back and forth slowly. "That's all it said. I have to admit, it did make me wonder about the people that built that gigantic house. Do you think she was their daughter? I wonder when she was born. I wish they had put the date." Patty's interest was growing by the minute. Tosha told Patty that there was not a lot of information at the library about the family, but that her mom was going to help her get more information. Tosha was pleased that Patty seemed curious about the whole thing. She was now more determined than ever to explore this house, and wanted to do it with her cousin.

Tosha made it all sound so exciting. Nothing seemed scary when her cousin talked about it, and Patty did have to retrieve her backpack. "Well, I suppose we could do a little exploring." Together, the cousin's made plans for the next day. If the rain would just stop, tomorrow they would be inside Graybrook.

The next day was clear and bright. Early that morning, they asked Patty's mom if they could pack a lunch and go to Angelica's house for the afternoon. Her mom agreed, and she helped them pack their lunch, but insisted they include Lori Lynn in their plans for later that day. "You can't leave your sister out of everything for the entire week. You have to let her play with you and Tosha once in a while," Patty's mom said, and both girls quickly agreed.

The girls gathered up the lunch, and Tosha put it in her backpack. They were relieved to finally be on their way. This time it seemed like they reached the mansion much quicker. Patty was starting to feel a little nervous, but she kept it to herself.

They knew exactly where to find the opening in the fence and headed straight for it. Walking across the big lawn didn't take them long either. Tosha stepped onto the patio without hesitation, but not Patty. She hung back, remembering the skunk that greeted her the last time she was here. She definitely didn't want that to happen again.

Tosha misread her cousin's reluctance. "Patty, you said you wanted to do this. Don't get cold feet already." Then Tosha realized her cousin's eyes were focused on the bushes near the patio door. "Oh, the skunk! Patty he's long gone, don't worry about him."

Patty slowly walked over and joined her cousin. As they found themselves standing on the patio, they stopped and looked at each other with a mixture of excitement and apprehension in their eyes.

Tosha asked Patty to show her the baby's footprints she had found in the cement on her previous visit. Patty took her over to the edge near the door where she had fallen. Tosha was even more moved than Patty when she looked down at the tiny footprints and the inscription. She knelt down just as Patty had and with her fingertips, lightly brushed the lose dirt off the imprint. "Patty, they are so little and so sweet. It makes me wish I could have met her."

"Yes, it makes me feel the same way," Patty agreed.

Tosha stood up and both girls walked the few steps over to the patio door. Patty noticed it was slightly open. Tosha was the one to reach for the door first. As she started to push it open Patty stopped her. Tosha saw the visible fear in her cousin's eyes. In a pleading tone Patty said, "Tosha, before we do this, promise me you won't leave me alone. Promise that we will stay together no matter what, okay?"

Tosha gave her cousin a little impatient look. "Of course we'll stay together, I promise. Don't worry so much, this will be fun."

This time both girls reached for the door, and together pushed it open. It didn't even squeak. They entered the house, taking only a few steps before stopping. Patty spotted her backpack setting on the floor right where she had fallen. Eagerly she bent over and scooped it up. She unzipped it and rummaged inside to verify its contents. Satisfied and greatly relieved, she let out a big sigh. "It's here. Everything is here." Holding it close to her, she hugged it tightly. She was so happy to have it back in her own hands again.

Tosha did not observe her cousin's joy at having her backpack and library book once again in her possession. Instead she was filling her eyes with every inch of the interior of the room they were standing in. It was large, and full of sunlight. Tosha was sure it was an interior sun room or patio room. She stepped over, took Patty's hand, and slowly started toward the next room, taking Patty along with her.

The house was so big and so still that every footstep echoed loudly throughout the room. Patty silently wished she had worn her tennis shoes instead of sandals. Leaving the patio room, they walked on deeper inside the mansion. The further they went into the house, the darker it became. The second large room they came to, they had to pause to allow their eyes time to adjust to the dim light. Heavy draperies covered the windows, giving the room a gloomy feeling. Their feet seemed stuck to the floor. Neither one of them knew what to do next. It was as if they were in a movie, it all seemed so unreal. So far, the house had no furniture at all, not even as much as a wall-hanging or picture. It appeared nothing had been left behind. Tosha was very disappointed at the emptiness of it all, but was far from giving up hope. After all, this was a really big house with many rooms. They would surely find something interesting somewhere.

The girls cautiously made their way through the house. Each room had the same empty look about it. There were no traces of the people who once lived there.

The house seemed harmless enough. Patty was just beginning to relax when they came to a very large open area. This looked like the front of the house. To one side of them was a pair of tall doors. Patty thought they must be the main doors to the house. Directly across from the doors was the biggest staircase Patty had ever seen in her life. It was so wide that ten people could walk up it side by side. The staircase curved slowly as it went up, up, up, so far that the girls could not see where it ended.

Tosha was fascinated. "Patty, isn't this the coolest thing ever? I've never seen anything so big. Not even the museum downtown has a staircase this huge." Patty knew Tosha would want to go upstairs. She felt herself losing all her courage. She grabbed Tosha's hand and held on tightly. They started up the staircase, both looking into the darkness that loomed above them. Patty felt her heart pounding in her chest. She closed her eyes tightly and allowed her cousin to pull her along, only opening them a tiny bit every now and then.

Tosha felt herself drawn up the stairs. She desperately wanted to find *something* that would give her some clues about the family who had lived here. She had so many questions. She was sure if anything had been left behind, it would be in the attic.

Tosha was headed for the top and there was no stopping her. When they reached the second floor they paused for a moment, and then continued on to the next level, the third floor. It seemed to Patty that the higher they went up the stairs, the gloomier it became. The house was so still that the only thing she could hear was their own breathing and the echo of their footsteps. There was no carpet anywhere, only the hard cold floors that picked up their shadows as they walked along. Eventually all the shadows vanished, leaving in their place an eerie blackness. Patty could hardly tell when they'd reached the top floor. The fact that her eyes had been shut most of the way up the stairs didn't help.

Tosha hesitated at the top of the stairs, trying to decide which way to go first. After only a few seconds, she headed down the dark hallway way to their left, pulling her timid cousin along with her.

Tosha stopped unexpectedly, and Patty felt her body tense up. Patty squeezed her eyes closed even tighter. She was afraid to open them, but when she heard Tosha let out a small gasp and felt Tosha's hand tighten down on her own, that did it. Startled, Patty's eyes flew open. The shadowy sight that loomed before her caused her mouth to fly open. The whole house shook with the sound of her screams. Looking down the dim hallway, she could barely make out the tall figure of a man. He was taller than any man she had ever seen. He appeared to have horns on the top of his head, and two more on his shoulders. He had no face, and at his side was a long knife. He stood very straight and did not move or speak to them.

This was way worse than the skunk, Patty thought. She had never known such terror. Still holding Tosha's hand, she headed for the stairs in a dead run, dragging Tosha along with her. When they reached the railing of the staircase, Tosha grabbed hold and held on tight, nearly jerking Patty off her feet, and almost causing Patty to go head first down the long staircase. Tosha held on to Patty tightly, trying to steady her. Their arms flew around each other.

The only sound that remained in the hallway was their heavy breathing. Tosha could hear Patty gasping for air, and realized she was having a total panic attack. Tosha had to get her calmed down. They sat on the floor at the top of the steps, still holding onto each other in silence. They had hardly said a word to each other since entering the house, but their silence was broken now. Patty's voice was only a whisper, as if talking aloud would awake the giant man. There was true fear in her voice. "Tosha, that was a man I just saw standing in the hallway. I know you saw him too. We've got to get out of here."

Tosha had seen the figure, and yes, it did startle her a little, but she was sure it was not a man. Tosha said with complete certainty, "Patty, it's not a man. Think about it. Why would a man be in this big empty house all alone? No one is here except you and me."

Patty was amazed by her cousin's calmness. "Tosha, what makes you so sure? We have to get out of here. Please, let's leave right now. I have a bad feeling about this place!"

Tosha was determined to explore the house further. She knew it would be hard to get Patty to come back once they left. With a soft but stern voice Tosha said, "Patty, let's just sit here a minute. You'll be fine. We are not leaving yet! We promised each other we would stay together, so you can't leave without me, and I can't leave without you. Anyway, if that was a man back there, why isn't he coming after us?" Tosha asked, raising her shoulders questioningly.

Patty looked over at her cousin in total frustration. "Tosha, what do you think you're going to find? This is crazy! What makes you so sure that's not a man back there? It sure looked like one to me. He's probably waiting for us right now. Why don't we just leave, go home, and forget all about this old mansion," Patty finished feeling exhausted.

Tosha let out a big sigh. She looked around in the gloom that surrounded them. She sounded wishful as she spoke. "I don't know what I'm looking for. I just want to know more about this place. I can't explain it. It's as if something is pulling me along, guiding my steps. I just have this strong feeling that we're going to discover something wonderful. I can't leave just yet. We have to look through the whole house. I know you're afraid, but aren't you a little curious too?"

Without hesitation Patty replied, "No, I'm too creeped out to be curious, but I'm not going downstairs without you. We're on the last floor, right?" Patty saw her cousin nodding her head in acknowledgment. "Okay then, we will check out the rest of this floor and then leave. Okay?" Once again Patty saw Tosha's head nodding up and down in an eager response.

"Yes," Tosha said as she stood up. "This is the last floor. Let's look around and then we'll go home." Tosha waved her hand in the dim light and Patty could tell she was motioning her to follow.

Standing up, Patty fell in step behind her cousin. "Tosha," Patty whispered, "let's go a different way. I don't want to go back down the hall where that tall giant is."

"Patty, I think we should check it out. I want to prove to you that it is not a giant or a man. You don't even have to look at it, I'll do that part. Just follow me and keep your eyes closed if it makes you feel better."

Patty couldn't believe her cousin really wanted a closer look at whatever was standing in the dark hall, but she knew her cousin well enough to know that there was no stopping her. Patty worked hard to regain some of her courage as she followed Tosha down the hallway.

Slowly they approached the stiff figure standing up against the wall. It had not moved one inch from where they had first spotted it. This helped confirm Tosha's suspicions.

There was so little light, Tosha couldn't see very well. Patty kept pulling at Tosha as if trying to hold her back. Clearly she didn't want to get very close to the figure. All this was making it very hard for Tosha to get a good look at it. Suddenly, Tosha remembered something. Why hadn't she thought of it before? She pulled her backpack off her shoulder and dug around inside until her fingers found what they were searching for. She pulled her hand from her backpack. All at once there was light in the hallway. Tosha had retrieved her flashlight. Patty loved the idea and immediately found her flashlight too. Both girls shined their lights on the figure before them.

Tosha was intrigued by what she saw. Her suspicions were wrong. She thought the figure might be a statue of some kind, but this was much better. It was a suit of armor, she had read about them. She explained to Patty what they were looking at. "This is a suit of armor, Patty. We just studied about them last year. Warriors wore them to protect themselves in battle long ago. It must be three or four-hundred years old. This is the coolest thing I've ever seen in my whole life."

Patty thought it was the spookiest thing she'd ever seen, and was uncomfortable even standing this close to it. The armor had a strange helmet that was pointed on top. It held an enormous round shield in one hand and a long sword in the other. There were sharp spikes on each of his shoulders, and the entire thing was covered with spider webs and thick dust. Patty took several steps backward, pulling Tosha with her. She wanted to put a little more space between them and it.

Softly, Patty asked, "Do you think someone could be inside it? There is a cover over where the face should be."

Tosha almost laughed out loud, "Yeah, right! There's a three-hundred year old man standing in this dusty, dark, suit of armor, just waiting for us to come along. If you want, we could lift the face-cover up and see if he's still alive?" Tosha pretended to step closer to the armor.

Instantly Patty jumped backward, putting even more distance between her and the armor. Tosha started to giggle. She just couldn't hold it back any longer.

Patty turned a serious face toward her cousin. "That isn't funny. No way are we going to touch that thing, no way!"

"Okay, okay, don't get excited. I was just kidding. You have to admit though, it is really cool looking!"

"I don't have to admit anything," Patty commented coolly as she started tugging on Tosha's hand, backing away even further from the tall iron man. Unexpectedly, Patty lost her balance and both girls got tangled up in each other's feet. Down to the floor they went, with backpacks and flashlights scattering. Without hesitation, both girls reached for their flashlights and searched for other items that had fallen out of their backpacks.

Tosha had crawled some distance across the floor to retrieve one of her books, when she noticed this part of the hallway seemed to have more light. She looked around trying to discover where the light was coming from, and noticed a door. It was partially open, and she realized that had to be where the light was coming from.

Patty was collecting the last of her things when, from behind her, she heard Tosha scream. A rush of footsteps, then the loud bang of a slamming door quickly followed. Patty could feel the hair on the back of her neck stand up.

She was afraid to turn around. Her legs felt like they had turned to water. She was sure something terrible had happened to her cousin. She quickly and quietly melted to the floor and crouched down on her knees. She wanted to make herself as small as possible. She turned off her flashlight, and worked to quiet her breathing. Holding on tightly to her backpack, her mind raced wondering what she should do next.

She knew the first thing to do was to stop shaking. Fear ran up Patty's back like a cold wind. She felt her teeth chattering and was sure the sound of them could be heard everywhere in the big house. Huddled in the gloomy hallway, Patty struggled to put her thoughts together. It was dark, but she was afraid to turn her flashlight back on. Taking in several deep, slow breaths, she realized what she had to do. She had to search for her cousin.

Slowly, Patty eased her way to a standing position. 'Okay', she said to herself, the sounds I heard came from behind me. She turned and faced that direction. "Tosha," she whispered. Patty stopped and scolded herself. I can do better, she thought. She summoned all the courage she could find. Pulling her shoulders back and straightening to her full height, she cleared her throat and spoke in a clearer, stronger voice. "Tosha, can you hear me?"

Her voice echoed back to her. She waited, hoping that Tosha would call back, but she didn't.

She commanded her feet to move forward one step at a time. She had no idea what lay ahead of her, but she knew she wasn't leaving the mansion without her cousin. She would find her, she had to find her! Her mind filled with a number of images. The worst was that her cousin was being held captive by the man wearing the armor. Or, maybe she had fallen through a trap door and tumbled down to the cellar. Patty slammed her eyes shut. She had to clear her mind, to find a way to control her imagination.

When she opened her eyes, to her amazement, she saw the faint outline of a door in the shadows. With her flashlight gripped tightly in her hand, she switched it on. To her relief, she could now see the door clearly. Her feet felt like lead as she forced them to move closer to the door. Now, standing only a couple of feet from it, Patty cautiously reached out her trembling hand for the doorknob, not knowing what she would find on the other side. For Patty, this was one of the scariest things she'd ever done.

With her hand only inches from the ominous doorknob, Patty's outstretched hand froze with new-found terror. Standing like a stone statue, she watched the doorknob start to turn all by itself. This was more than she could take. Her screams came one right after another. She turned to run for the stairs. Patty could hear her own footsteps racing down the hall. They sounded so loud. Suddenly, she realized that someone or something was chasing her. With new-found energy she surged forward. She could see the top of the staircase just ahead of her. Then she felt something grab her by the ankle and she fell to the floor. Kicking and screaming with all her might, Patty fought to free herself. Mingled in with her own screams, Patty was shocked to hear her cousin's voice yelling at her.

"Patty, stop kicking me! I'm sorry if I scared you. I didn't mean to, really." Tosha yelled while holding up her hands to protect herself against her cousin's impressive efforts to defend herself.

Patty's eyes, which had been shut throughout the struggle, flew open. "Tosha!" Patty exclaimed, "I thought something awful had happened to you!" Patty's arms flew up and she grabbed her cousin in a tight hug. "I was coming to find you, to rescue you. I was scared to death. I heard you scream." Patty let go of Tosha, but continued to jabber. With her hands flapping around in the air she asked, "What happened to you? Where did you disappear to?"

Tosha reached out for her cousin's hands and grabbed hold of them tightly. "Patty, I found something amazing. It's the attic. You've got to come see it. Come on! Come on and let me show you." Patty pulled her hands free from her cousin's. She was still shaken by the whole episode and was not ready to run off exploring, especially in some dark, dusty old attic.

Tosha saw the frustrated look in her cousin's eyes and apologized again. "I said I was sorry. I just saw the door and looked in. When I realized it was the attic, I got so excited. I guess I must have screamed, and then I ran up the attic steps before I could even think. I must have somehow bumped the door and caused it to slam. I didn't do it on purpose, honest." Tosha held her hands out in a pleading gesture. "I was only gone for a minute...or...two. I just wanted to take a quick peek to see if there was anything up there," Tosha continued, trying to explain. She knew Patty was really unhappy with her and she knew she shouldn't have left her all alone in the hall, but Tosha just couldn't help herself.

"Come on Patty, you've got to come see it. You'll love it, really you will! It's not scary at all. There are lots and lots of big windows that fill the attic with sunlight. It's huge! Come on, let me show you. There are shelves and large boxes of stuff. Just think of all the neat things that might be in them. Once we check out this room, I promise, we will go home."

# CHAPTER THREE

# THE TRUNK

Patty had to admit it might be fun looking through the boxes. She also knew there was no way Tosha would leave now that she had finally found something interesting to explore.

Patty gave in to Tosha's coaxing with a shrug of her shoulders. She shook her head and said, "Okay, okay, but I'm still mad at you for running off like that."

"It won't happen again, I promise. Just do this with me and I won't bug you again," Tosha said, wearing a winning smile. Her eyes sparkled with anticipation of the new adventure in the attic. "Come on, let's go."

Flashlights once again in hand, they went down the hallway, through the door and up the long narrow staircase. Patty was surprised to find the large open attic so full of light, just as Tosha had said. The attic wasn't scary at all. In fact, it was almost cheerful. She could feel herself relaxing.

They both surveyed the layout of the attic, trying to decide where to start first. They tucked their flashlights away and started looking around. On one side of the attic rested tall cabinets. On the other side there were several boxes scattered on the floor. "Let's just start looking around and see what we can find. But if you find something awesome, let me know, okay?" Tosha suggested, wiggling her fingers as she gazed at the boxes on the floor. She was obviously itching to get started.

"Good idea," Patty replied, eyeing the cabinets along the far wall. The girls split up and walked in separate directions.

Tosha was glad that her cousin seemed much better here in the attic, and what luck that this was the place where there was so much to explore. Tosha went over and sat on the floor in front of the boxes. She opened the first one and started pulling out each and every item.

Patty approached the cabinets with interest. There were seven of them and they were at least six feet tall with dozens of doors covering them. The first one she opened caused an unexpected gasp to escape her throat. The cabinet was full of books, hundreds of books.

Tosha had pulled out several items when she came to an envelope, it was yellowed with age. She reached for it and was holding it in her hand when she heard her cousin. Tosha's head spun around, "What is it Patty, did you find something?"

"Yeah, these cabinets are full of books, tons of them." Patty was overjoyed, she loved books.

Tosha stood up and walked over to where Patty was standing. She had her head tipped back and was looking all the way to the top of the open bookcase. Assorted sizes and colors of dark muted books were lined up neatly. Tosha stepped over to the next cabinet and opened it. It was full of books too. "Wow!" Tosha exclaimed. There are more books here than there are at the public library. Do you think it would be okay if we borrowed some of them?"

Patty was in awe, "I don't know, maybe." She pulled her eyes away and looked at her cousin. "Tosha, I didn't think we'd find anything this cool. Did you find anything in the boxes?" Patty noticed the envelope in her cousin's hand. "What's that?" She asked pointing at Tosha's hand.

"Oh, I don't know. Let me see." Tosha took the envelope and turned it over. She was happy to discover it had not been sealed. She gently pulled it open and peered inside. "Wow, it's a key, a really old-looking key. I wonder what it opens." Tosha gazed down at the small key, turning it over and over in her hand. For being old, it was remarkably shiny. "It's so pretty, it looks more like a charm from a bracelet than a key that actually opens something."

Patty had lost interest in what her cousin had found. She decided to look in the remaining cabinets. They were way better than an old key. The fifth cabinet that she opened had books on the upper shelves, but it was what she saw in the bottom of the cabinet that caused Patty to blurt out a small scream of delight, "Wow, look at this Tosha!"

Tosha nearly dropped the key when she heard her cousin scream. She jerked her head up and ran over to where Patty stood in front of another bookcase. Her eyes grew large with excitement as she looked at what seemed to be a huge old steamer trunk. "Oh Patty, this is *so* cool!" It had been tucked away out of sight. Tosha was delighted to see how excited Patty was at finding this magnificent treasure. This trunk was bound to be full of some very special stuff. "Come on, help me pull it out," she said to her cousin, while absent-mindedly slipping the small key into her jeans pocket.

Together, the girls wrapped their arms around the trunk and, using all their strength, pulled hard. It was heavy, but they were rewarded when at last they felt it slip out from its hiding place. At first they just walked around it, looking it over. The surface of the trunk was very rough and was covered with thick dust. It was a dark brown, and had lots of scuffs and scratches on it. "I'd say this trunk has been used a lot over the years," Tosha observed. She couldn't help but wonder about the many interesting places the person who had owned it might have traveled to. There were large strips of leather at the corners and across the top of it. Tosha noticed two long slits across the top, and it had leather handles on each end. When they came around to the front, they noticed it had a small tarnished lock on it. The girls slowly sank down to their knees.

"Now what are we going to do," Patty asked in a frustrated voice.

"I don't know, we could try to find something to break it. It's small so it shouldn't be too hard, but I don't want to do that. In the movies I've seen them pick locks, but I don't know how to do it. Oh darn, I want to see what's inside. I wonder if we could find the key for it...Oh wait!" Tosha stood up and reached her hand into her jeans pocket. "Could we be so lucky...?" She leaned down beside her cousin. Holding her breath she slowly held the key up to the lock, lined it up, and slipped it in. "It fits!"

"But will it open it? Go on...try it!" Patty urged.

Tosha got a firm grip on the key and slowly turned it. Both girls heard the click and saw the lock snap open. All they could do was look at each other with open mouths formed in a wordless, 'WOW.' To Tosha's surprise, it was Patty who stood up and reached for the lid first.

Patty had been watching every move Tosha made. She found herself just as curious as her cousin was about finding something like this. She couldn't wait to see what was inside. Patty's hands were shaking as she touched the lid, and her fingers fumbled to get a hold of it. Without a word, Tosha stood up and put her hands next to Patty's, and together the girls lifted the lid of the old trunk. The cracking and groaning sound the lid made was so loud in the silence of the attic that both girls shivered. The trunk was very large so they had to stand on their tiptoes to get the lid open all the way. They both gazed down into the open trunk, eager to explore the contents of it. They were shocked to see only one small box in the bottom.

Tosha let out a disappointed sigh. "Oh no, that's all that's in it? It's such a big trunk, how can that be?" she complained.

Patty wasn't disappointed quite so easily. She was already reaching for the little box. The trunk was so big it was a long reach. Bending down over the edge of the trunk, she stretched her body and her fingers out as far as possible, but she couldn't reach it. Losing her balance, she nearly fell in the trunk. Having lost all sense of fear, she decided to climb inside. Once there, she bent down and picked up the box. Gently she held it, as if it were a fragile treasure. It looked old. The edges were tattered and yellowed with age. Patty cautiously opened the box. She heard a small gasp escape her own lips as she gazed down at the most beautiful book she had ever seen in her life. The cover was deep red with gold trim around the edges. She slowly turned the book over to look at the back side of it. There were no words printed on it anywhere. Patty was so engrossed in it that she unconsciously sat down inside the large roomy trunk. Making herself comfortable, she continued to examine her new-found treasure.

Tosha had walked back over to the box she had been looking through before. She decided to finish looking through it. She glanced over her shoulder to see what Patty was doing, and realized she had disappeared. Tosha instantly ran back to the trunk. "Patty, where are you?" Tosha called out. She reached the trunk and peered down inside it. "What are you doing inside the trunk? I thought something happened to you!"

Patty looked up at her cousin with a big smile on her face. She held the book up and replied, "Look what I found. I think it's a journal, or a diary. It's full of hand-written pages."

Tosha's eyes locked onto the book with renewed interest. She climbed over the edge and joined her cousin inside the trunk. Both girls inspected the red and gold book, so happy that they had finally found something. "A diary, really! This might give us some clues about the people who lived here. Does it have a title?" Tosha asked.

Patty flipped back to the first page, and her breath caught in her throat. The first page had markings that looked like Egyptian symbols. Under the markings were the words, '*TRAVEL DIARY.*' Thrilled, the two cousins looked at each other. Using her thumb, Patty fanned through countless pages. The hand written entries were in bold black ink and all in the same handwriting. Patty stopped somewhere near the middle, and started reading.

They were just getting started ,when from somewhere above them they heard an awful sound. It was a loud bang, followed by a scraping noise. The girls were so engrossed in the diary that the unexpected noise caused them to jump so hard the lid on the trunk slammed down, closing them inside. Immediately, Tosha wanted to open the lid. As she reached to push it open, Patty grabbed her by the arm. Quietly, as if someone might hear her, Patty said to Tosha, "Let's leave it shut, if anyone is out there they will never find us in here. Let's just stay here and see if we hear anything else."

This made sense to Tosha. She looked up and noticed sunlight streaming in through the two slits in the lid she had seen earlier. Tosha settled back down in the now semi-dark trunk. They both sat very still, listening intently for any other sounds. After several minutes of complete silence, Tosha found herself once again digging for her flashlight. Patty followed her example, and with both flashlights shining, the trunk became a very pleasant little hide-a-way.

Patty was still listening with a worried frown on her face, concerned about what might be out there.

Tosha slipped the diary from Patty's hands, and began softly reading from it.

*Today was a very exciting day for the archeologist and his young daughter. A fantastic discovery for any archeologist, they unearthed one of the largest tombs on record. There were countless chambers and tunnels. There is much to explore, so they will be here for quite awhile. His daughter loves this country. She finds the people interesting, but the climate strange, hot in the daytime, and very cold at night. The huge sand dunes are beautiful, and the sand itself is unlike anything she's ever seen. It's so fine, it feels more like powder than sand.*

As Tosha read on, her younger cousin relaxed and became so wrapped up in what Tosha was reading, she forgot all about the scary sound from somewhere in the attic. She even forgot about being in the attic, or that she was in a big trunk. She was so drawn into the writings of the journal that she could imagine what the sand felt like. She could feel the heat of the sun, and smell the gentle breeze drifting across the desert.

After a while, Tosha felt a great need to stand and stretch. She had been reading for at least twenty minutes. As she stood up, she pushed the lid open. Patty reached up, taking the diary from her cousin's hand. She wanted to start reading where her cousin had left off. Suddenly, the trunk was full of intense light and a breeze swirled around her face, blowing her hair. In total surprise and confusion Patty looked up to see what had happened to cause such a change. She looked up to see Tosha's face wearing a look of total astonishment. Tosha's hair was blowing too, and flying all around her face. She had raised her hand and was holding it above her eyes, as if shielding them from the sun. Her mouth hung open in wonder as she looked around.

Patty tensed up, something was very wrong. Maybe someone was in the attic, or maybe the sound they heard earlier was an attic window, breaking. That would explain the wind, but not the brightness of sunlight. Out of reflex Patty reached up, grabbing Tosha's hand to pull her back down into the trunk. This unexpected force caused Tosha to lose her balance and fall backwards into the trunk. The lid slammed shut. Now both girls again sat in the depths of the trunk.

Patty could hear her cousin breathing very hard. She even thought she could feel Tosha trembling, causing the entire trunk to shake. She had never seen her normally calm cousin so upset, and it was very unsettling to Patty. She didn't know what to do. Too frightened to speak, her mind raced as she sat in silence. Then Tosha reached for her flashlight that had fallen to the bottom of the trunk. Urgently she snatched the diary off of Patty's lap. With a frown on her face, Patty wondered what Tosha was up to. Finally, Patty found her voice. "Tosha, what are you doing? What did you see out there? Tell me what is happening!" Patty pleaded.

Tosha was too distracted to respond to her cousin's questions. Her hands shook as they looked at the last page that she had read. Now re-reading it out loud, her voice was just a whisper.

*Her father promised her they would stay at the Inn tonight. A welcome change from the tent they had called home for the past weeks. Staying at the Inn would mean a nice hot bath. She felt long overdue for such a luxury. Her small pet monkey, Chatters, who is always welcome at the dig sites, will also be welcome at the inn. Her father was treated like royalty in this part of the world and the small monkey, though sometimes mischievous, is a very well behaved pet.*

*Today had been a wonderful day. Her father had taken some time away from the dig and took both Emma and Chatters to the marketplace. The marketplace was one of her favorite things about this part of the world.*

Tosha stopped reading, laying the diary in her lap. Patty saw the puzzled look on her cousin's face. Then suddenly Tosha seemed to brighten up. "I've got it! I think I know what has happened! Patty, you're not going to believe this!" Tosha's voice was full of excitement.

Patty was getting frustrated with her cousin. She looked at Tosha and once again asked, "What are you talking about? What did you see? You are scaring me to death! There's someone out there, isn't there? Someone is in the mansion?"

Tosha laughed at that remark. "Well, you're half right; I think it's safe to say someone is out there all right. There are a whole lot of people out there. Really, something amazing has happened. It's okay, you're just going to have to see it to believe it. Go ahead, just take a little peek. Don't be afraid. Come on, I'll do it with you," Tosha said in a relaxed voice. She no longer seemed scared. She was more like her old self.

"What on earth are you jabbering about? What people? That can't be. We're in the attic, remember. Maybe I don't want to look out there after seeing the expression on your face a moment ago, you looked terrified!" Patty was beginning to think her cousin was losing her mind.

"Well, I suppose I was a little bit scared, but now I've figured out what's happened. Come on Patty, let's just take a quick peek outside the trunk. I'm not kidding, it's amazing. You're going to love it, just look!"

Patty thought Tosha was up to something. "You better not be playing a trick on me! Okay Tosha, I'll look, but if it's another suit-of-armor or something spooky like that, I'm going home, with or without you!"

Together both girls lifted the lid just enough to see out. Patty was totally spellbound. It was almost impossible for her to comprehend the fact that, indeed, they were definitely not in the attic. They were sitting right in the middle of what appeared to be an open-air market, but this was unlike any market place she had ever seen. Her mom and dad had taken her and her sister to the City Market downtown. Patty had thought it was rather boring, but it was nothing like this, this place was anything but boring. All around them, people walked by dressed in long white robe-dresses, even the men. Along both sides of the dirt street sat strange tables with funny looking roofs over them. The tables were piled high with colorful fruits, fabrics, and hats of all sorts. There were cages with parrots and snakes. There was even one with monkeys in it. The air was full of assorted smells, not all of them good.

Patty and Tosha were completely taken in by their surroundings. Tosha started pointing things out to Patty, and Patty was doing the same to Tosha. It was amazing!

"Oh Patty," Tosha said, "Look at that camel. I've never seen one with a carriage on top of it before, have you?" The camel had a structure on its back that resembled a small carriage. It had an elegant seat covered with thick cushions. There was a fancy roof over the top of it and large tassels dangled from each corner. It was obviously for someone very rich, or important.

Patty squealed with delight, "Tosha, look at those adorable little monkeys. Aren't they cute?"

There was so much going on. Everywhere they looked there was something else interesting to see. Then Patty spotted a little girl. She looked to be about eight or nine years old. What really caught Patty's eye was that this girl seemed so out of place. She watched every move the girl made as she gracefully walked through the market. The dress she wore was beautiful. It was made of a pale lace that hung clear to her ankles and swayed as she walked along the road. Atop her head sat a wide floppy hat made of the same lacy fabric as her dress. Patty saw the girl stop and turn to give her attention to a tiny monkey with a white face. She bent down and lifted the monkey up into her arms. Patty watched her shake her finger at him, gently scolding him. He had the sweetest little round face that moved back and forth, taking in every passer-by. He seemed to almost smile as he looked at the girl who was holding him so protectively. Patty couldn't pull her eyes from them.

Tosha followed her cousin's gaze, and together they watched the young girl and her tiny companion. "Patty, are you having fun? I was afraid you would go into shock when you realized what had happened to us. Instead, you seem to be having a good time."

Patty was so curious and so interested in what she was looking at, that she seemed to have forgotten everything else, including Tosha, until now. She felt herself being pulled down inside the trunk.

Patty's face was crowded with a mixture of emotions; wonder, excitement, confusion, and even joy. She looked over at her cousin, "Tosha, where do you think we are, and how did we get here? Did you see the funny-looking clothes those people were wearing, and did you see all those big tents? They don't look anything like the ones we camp in." With excitement in her eyes, Patty reached up and raised the trunk lid. She just had to take another look. She was greeted by a big commotion going on just outside the trunk. A merchant was running through the street chasing a little monkey. The monkey was darting back and forth among the shoppers. Then, all of a sudden, both the monkey and the merchant turned and headed right for them. Frightened, Patty slammed the lid down tight with a loud bang. This was followed by some heavy bumps and a loud scolding in a foreign language. The trunk bounced around and the lid flapped letting in sunshine and a fair amount of dust.

"Oh my gosh, Tosha. Something is going on out there. I think that little monkey we saw a moment ago, is in some sort of trouble. Maybe we should see if we can help him." Patty was jumping around in the trunk. Everything was in chaos.

Tosha reached out and put her hand over Patty's mouth to silence her. "Patty, stop worrying about the monkey. Settle down before you knock the whole trunk over. We have to figure out what to do. We can't just sit here in this trunk all day."

Patty's earlier expression was now replaced with a worried frown. She sat back in the trunk, realizing they had a big problem. "Tosha, where do you think we are? I still don't understand how we got here, do you?"

"Well," Tosha replied, "I'm not sure how we got here, but I think I know where we are. Here, look at this page in the diary. This is the part I was reading before I stopped and opened the trunk.

Patty took the diary from her cousin and started reading where Tosha had indicated.

*Her father promised her they would stay at the Inn tonight, a welcome change from the tent they had called home for the past weeks. Staying at the inn would mean a nice hot bath. She felt long overdue for such a luxury. Her small pet monkey, Chatters, who is always welcome at the dig sites, will also be welcome at the inn. Her father was treated like royalty in this part of the world and the small monkey, though sometimes mischievous, is a very well behaved pet. Today had been a wonderful day. Her father had taken some time away from the dig and took both Emma and Chatters to the marketplace. The marketplace was one of her favorite things about this part of the world.*

Patty stopped reading and gently laid the diary down, her face tense. "Tosha, I think you are right. It sounds as if we are at the very place the diary is describing, but how can that be?" Tosha could hear panic creeping into her cousin's voice.

Patty waited for an answer to her question. She could always count on her cousin to come up with some sort of an explanation. She was hopeful that Tosha could explain what was happening to them.

Unfortunately, Tosha wasn't nearly as confident in herself as her cousin. She had no idea how this could happen. She even wondered if it was really happening at all. Maybe they were having an incredible dream, however that didn't seem possible either. This whole thing was too real; the sounds, the smells. No, Tosha was certain that this was really happening.

Somehow they had traveled to the very spot they were reading about in the diary. Logic told her that if they turned the page and read about something or someplace different, they would just as likely end up at that place of description. So, now what do they do? Tosha had an idea. She picked up the diary and started to flip through the pages. She wondered if since the trunk and diary were found in the attic, there was a chance that the diary might have writings in it about the mansion. They could read that part and *bam*, they could get back home.

Patty could tell that Tosha was working on a solution. This gave her some comfort.

Tosha scanned the pages, flipping to the very last page of entry. However, what she found there completely unnerved her. As she read, she was mystified by the words that lay on the pages she was reading. Fear made her throat feel tight, but curiosity made her read on, as the reality of what she was reading sank in.

With flashlight in hand, Patty watched her cousin's face. She could see, at one point, Tosha was very deep in thought. Then, she saw her expression change to one of confusion. Patty was worried that they would never again see their families, never get back home. Closing her eyes, Patty decided to say a little prayer of hope. She just wanted to go home, to be in her own bedroom, and yes, even play with her little sister. She opened her eyes and glanced up to see Tosha wearing a look of shock and ......something else. Patty couldn't bear the silence any longer. "Tosha," Patty squealed out a little louder than she meant to. "What's the matter? What is it? You look like you've seen a ghost!"

Patty's sudden outburst startled Tosha. She pulled her unbelieving eyes from the page she was reading to look at her cousin. Tosha was shaking her head back and forth in disbelief. No words of explanation would come, so without a word, Tosha slowly handed the diary to Patty. Tosha's hands were shaking so badly that she almost dropped the diary in her cousin's lap.

Patty tipped her head to one side, peeking around the flashlight. Cautiously she took the tiny book and peered down at the pages. With a trembling finger Tosha pointed to the place where she wanted Patty to start reading. Obediently, Patty slowly read the words that were written on the pages. Her face reflected the same confusion her cousin's face had shown. She paused and flipped the pages back and forth, taking in every line that was written in the same handwriting as all the other entries in the diary. Now reading aloud, Patty's voice took on an astonished tone.

*This was a day of great adventure for the two cousins. They went back to Graybrook and this time they both went inside. The big old house was scary, but they were determined to explore it.*

Patty stopped and looked over at Tosha with horror on her face. Her hands were shaking as she asked her cousin, "What does this mean? We did not write in this diary, but the diary is talking about everything we've done since we found the mansion, or Graybrook, or whatever it's called. Tosha, I'm really scared." Patty dropped the diary and reached for her backpack. She pulled it to her chest, and unconsciously wrapped her arms around it, hugging it to her body. It felt warm and familiar. "This is just getting weirder by the minute. I don't understand any of it." With a fearful look on her face, Patty hung her head.

Tosha was still shaking. She felt bad. "Patty, this is my fault. I was the one who wanted to explore the old mansion, not you. I promise you, I will get us out of this mess." Tosha paused and took a deep breath. She couldn't explain it, but she knew everything was going to be okay. Tosha reached down and retrieved the diary from the floor of the trunk. "Patty, don't worry! Everything is going to work out. I just know it. I have this feeling that the trunk and diary are very special, maybe even magical! I don't think anything bad will happen to us, really I don't."

Patty's head snapped up. Looking at her cousin, Patty said, "What do you mean 'nothing bad'. Are you crazy? Look outside again. Remember where we are? How can you say nothing bad will happen when it already has? Here we are in some strange country with nothing but sand around us, and people we can't even understand."

Tosha thought for a moment and then decided to do exactly what Patty suggested and look outside the trunk.

Tosha started to get up and open the lid, when a strange noise screeched out so loudly that Tosha lost her balance and she fell back down. Slightly stunned, Tosha glanced over at Patty. Both girls were alarmed. "What was that?" Tosha asked.

Patty panicked and lost all control. She reached out and threw her arms around Tosha's neck, holding on for dear life, sure that her own life was about to come to an end. Patty's grip was so tight that Tosha couldn't breathe. She struggled with Patty to free herself. Both girls were kicking and screaming, bouncing around inside the trunk. It felt like a couple of extra passengers were in the trunk with them. Knees and elbows were flying, with pokes and gouges coming from every direction. Mixed in with their screams, were sounds of strange squeals and shrieking. Total panic took hold of both cousins.

When Tosha finally managed to free herself, she jumped up pushing the lid up with her, and she quickly climbed out of the trunk. Now standing outside of it, she glanced around her. Tosha could not believe her eyes. She felt shrieks of joy escape her throat.

Patty's eyes were shut tight. She knew Tosha had opened the trunk and jumped out. She was so afraid, she couldn't bear to look. Then, she heard Tosha's scream. A cold chill ran down Patty's back. She huddled down deep inside the trunk, wanting to become invisible. She just knew someone had snatched Tosha and she feared she would be next.

# CHAPTER FOUR

# HOME AT LAST

Patty was holding as still as her fear would allow her, so she was startled to hear her cousin's voice.

"Well," Tosha said, "are you going to stay in there all day, or are you coming home with me?"

As Tosha's words hit her ears Patty felt a surge of relief. She cautiously wondered if it could be true, were they really home? There was only one way to find out, and that would involve her opening her eyes. At first she peeked through narrow slits, while unconsciously her hands slipped away from the firm grip she had on her backpack. She slowly raised herself up onto her knees. Placing her hands on the top edge of the trunk, she saw Tosha standing above her. They were back at the mansion. Patty never thought she would be so happy to be in Graybrook's old, dusty attic. Her eyes now fully open, she jumped out of the trunk with great joy. She grabbed Tosha and jumped up and down screaming, "We're back, we're back! How did you do it Tosha? How did you get us back here?" Laughing, Patty didn't allow her cousin the opportunity to explain how she did it. She was so relieved to be safe and sound again, she didn't wait for an explanation. "So that's why you were screaming! You were excited that we got back! I thought that angry merchant at the marketplace had grabbed you, and figured he was just waiting for me to pop my head up so he could grab me too!"

They both let out a sigh of relief. They couldn't believe their luck. Just a short walk and they would be back at Patty's house. Everything would be back to normal as if nothing had ever happened, or so they thought.

Tosha wondered if her idea about the diary was correct and if that's really how they ended up back here, or if something else had caused them to return. For now, she allowed Patty to give her the credit. Tosha was just happy it was over. She didn't care right now how it happened.

"Tosha, you were right. The diary must be magical. It has the power to take you to far-away places, and then bring you back again, just like that. Not that I ever plan to do this again!"

While Patty was jabbering away, Tosha's mind filled with more questions. "Patty," Tosha said, "I think I'll take the diary home with us. I want to read it from beginning to end."

Patty didn't like that idea at all. She begged her cousin not to take it. "Tosha, please don't. You may disappear right from under my nose. What would I tell my mom if she asked where you were? *'Oh, she's somewhere out there traveling around the world, but don't worry mom, she'll show up!'*" Patty was shaking her head at Tosha, with a disapproving look on her face.

"Oh Patty, don't be silly. How can I travel anywhere if the trunk is here and I'm at your house? Everything will be fine. You'll see."

Patty threw her hands up in the air, "Okay, but remember, I told you so." Patty watched as Tosha took the diary and put it in the little box, carefully tucking it inside her backpack. Then Patty reached down inside the trunk and snatched up her backpack. "Boy, I must really be tired, my backpack feels twice as heavy. What time is it anyway?" Patty was sure they had been gone for hours, it certainly felt like it to her.

Tosha looked at her watch, her nose wrinkled in thought. She shook her watch hand, still frowning. Then, with her fingertip, she tapped on the watch-face. "Patty," Tosha asked, "what time was it when we left your house?"

Patty thought for a minute, "I think it was around 11:00. Why?"

"Because," Tosha replied, "according to my watch, it's now 11:45. That means we've only been gone for about 45 minutes, and that's impossible. I wonder if my watch is broken."

"Maybe it is," Patty said as she peered down at her cousin's watch.

The girls made their way down the stairs with a newfound feeling of freedom. They raced each other to the patio doors, pulling the picnic lunch out of Tosha's backpack on their way out. Leaving the house behind them was a good feeling.

Tosha felt they had indeed discovered something amazing here today. This house had a magical feeling about it. She was fascinated by the house and so relieved to be back, she began enthusiastically talking about all that had happened to them.

With backpacks over one shoulder, and the lunch being carried between them, they headed for home.

"I'm hungry," Patty said.

"Me too," Tosha agreed.

Walking along, they each took turns dipping into the lunch, talking about their adventure, and trying to figure out an explanation for some of the strange events of the day.

# CHAPTER FIVE

# MONKEY BUSINESS

Patty had not noticed the tiny movements going on inside her backpack. She reached in the lunch bag and pulled out a banana. As she started peeling it, she heard Tosha let out a scream of surprise. This caused Patty to stop in mid-step. With a frown on her face, Patty looked over at her cousin to see what was causing this reaction. Hadn't they had enough screaming for one day? Patty changed her mind when she saw the look on Tosha's face and the shock in her eyes, focused right on Patty. Her mouth was wide open, and her finger was pointing at Patty. It was clear that Tosha was trying to warn her about something, but what?

Patty swirled around thinking that something was behind her. Now, with her back to Tosha, Patty was inspecting the area that had been directly behind her. Satisfied that nothing or no one was there, she whirled back around, ready to scold her cousin for scaring her that way. Before Patty could get out one word, Tosha started giggling hysterically. Patty watched as her cousin dropped to the ground and rolled with laughter, the kind that couldn't be stopped, no matter how badly you wanted it to.

Growing impatient with her cousin, Patty put her hands on her hips and glared at Tosha. She was struggling to regain enough control to explain her sudden outburst. Finding her voice, working hard to form each word, Tosha said, "Patty, you have...a...a...monkey coming out of your backpack!"

Patty froze, she wasn't sure whether to believe Tosha or not. How could she have a monkey in her backpack? Just about the time she started to question Tosha, Patty felt something crawling on her shoulder and then up on top of her head. Then she heard him. "Eeek, eeek," he screeched, wrapping his tail around Patty's chin to balance himself atop her head. Patty's eyes grew huge with surprise as they looked up toward the top of her head. She brought her hands up slowly to gently touch the stowaway that had claimed her head as his perch. Her eyes crossed as she tried to see the little monkey sitting on her head. "Oh my gosh," Patty exclaimed, as her hands grasped a hold of her newfound friend. She slowly brought him down into her arms. "Tosha, look at him. Isn't he cute! He looks just like the little monkey I saw with the girl at the marketplace. How in the world did he get in my backpack?"

Tosha watched the monkey snuggle in her cousin's arms. "I'll bet he's responsible for all the commotion when we heard that screeching noise that scared you so much. That also explains why it felt like there were three or four of us bouncing around inside the trunk...you know, when you were trying to choke me to death."

"I was NOT trying to choke you," Patty protested. "I was trying to hold on to you so we wouldn't fall out of the trunk. There was so much bumping and screaming going on, I was afraid." Patty stroked the monkey's soft fur. "I think I'll call him Chatters. That's the name of the little monkey in the diary. What do you think Tosha?"

"I don't care what you call him, I just want to know what we're going to tell your mom. Somehow, I don't think she's going to be very happy about this addition to your family," Tosha said, as her face took on a thoughtful look.

Patty's head shot up, "Oh no, what are we going to do? We have to take him home with us, but how are we going to explain it?" Patty wrapped her arms protectively around Chatters.

The girls stopped and sat down in the grass under a big shade tree. They needed time to think about what they were going to tell Patty's mom. "Tosha, what are we going to do?" Patty asked, looking at her older cousin for advice.

"Well, we could tell your mom that Chatters came running up to us as we were walking home from Angelica's house, and that we think he must be lost," Tosha offered.

Patty was happy with this story, because it wasn't a lie. Chatters had come out of nowhere, they were just leaving out the part about where they were when he ran to them. "Yeah, I like that."

Tosha wasn't sure how her cousin would respond to the next thing she wanted to talk about. "Patty, there is something else we need to discuss. We have to take Chatters back and I think we should do it right away, tomorrow."

Patty was holding him on her lap and patting him on top of his head. He was making soft little noises and wrapping his tail around Patty's wrist. When Patty heard Tosha's words, her hand stopped. Her head snapped up and looking at her cousin with disbelief on her face she said, "What are you talking about? Are you nuts?"

"You said yourself that you agreed with me," Tosha responded. "The diary must be magical, and it could take us anyplace that it had written about. You know Chatters doesn't belong here, he belongs back at the marketplace."

Patty had to agree that the adventure, now that it was over, had been a thrill, but it was also scary at times. Patty also agreed that Chatters really needed to be returned to his rightful place and Tosha *had* gotten them back home. She couldn't believe what she was about to say. "Okay, Tosha, I'll go back one more time." Patty was sure it was the right thing to do, and hoped she wouldn't be as scared this time.

After the three of them had some more lunch and their decision was made about what to do with the little monkey, they picked everything up and headed for home. Chatters was happy to ride home on Patty's shoulder, smacking his little mouth as he ate the rest of a cracker. Tosha could tell her cousin was as happy as could be with the little monkey on her shoulder. Patty had wanted a pet for a long time. Her parents had promised they would get her a dog someday, but 'someday' had not come yet.

Tosha glanced at her watch. It showed it was 12:00, it appeared to be working just fine now. "Patty, my watch seems to be working now. I sure hope it's right, because if it is, we'll be home right on time. It's as if time stood still while we were in the trunk!"

"Wow," Patty said, "wouldn't that be great? Just think, we could go anywhere the diary and trunk would take us and spend as much time there as we wanted to, and we could do it all without anyone missing us!"

Tosha stopped and looked at her cousin, "I can't believe my ears! Just this morning you swore you were never going back to Graybrook ever again!" Tosha said, amazed. "I practically had to drag you into the place. Now, you sound like you can't wait to go back, and not only that, you want to stay awhile."

Patty had lost all fear. She glanced at her cousin with a hurt look on her face. "That was before you figured out how the diary worked. Now we can come and go whenever we want, what could be better?"

Tosha just looked at her cousin and smiled an agreeing smile. She wasn't about to admit to Patty that she wasn't positive she had it *all* figured out, but the one thing she knew was that she wanted to go back to the attic again. She planned to study the diary tonight, and hopefully she *would* discover its secret. She couldn't wait to read it. She knew the answers were there, she just had to find them.

As they walked up the driveway to Patty's house, both girls felt nervous about the obvious questions they would be bombarded with. They had felt so sure of themselves and the story they invented, until Patty's house came into sight. The closer they got to the front door, the more fearful they became.

Tosha saw her own doubt reflected in her cousin's eyes. With confidence that she did not truly feel, she squeezed Patty's hand and gave her a big smile. "Everything will be fine, you'll see. Don't worry, okay?" Chatters must have sensed the girls' apprehension, because he climbed down and squeezed into Patty's backpack. His constant chattering had stopped.

As the girls walked into the house, they were very quiet. Tosha glanced over at the clock on the living room wall. It said 12:10. Wow, she thought to herself, time had stood still. The house was full of its usual commotion. Patty's mom was in the kitchen, cleaning. They could hear her dad in the backyard mowing, and Lori was probably playing on the swing set. The radio was playing one of her mom's favorite songs, filling the house with music. The girls said a quick 'hello' to Patty's mom and then ran to Patty's bedroom.

Once behind closed doors, Patty slid her backpack off and slowly opened the flap. "Come on Chatters," she softly coaxed. "Come on out. Everything is okay." Chatters popped his little head up and then happily jumped out and climbed straight up Patty's arm to sit on her shoulder. Patty looked at Tosha with a big smile on her face. "Isn't he the cutest thing ever? I wonder if mom would let me keep him," Patty said wishfully.

Tosha was sitting on Patty's bed observing Chatters as he played with the headband in Patty's hair. He seemed very much at home with his new master. Tosha knew how much Patty already loved this little guy. She hated to be the one to disappoint her cousin, but if not her, then surely Patty's mom would. "Patty," Tosha said, louder than she intended, "I thought we agreed to take him back!" Lowering her voice she continued, choosing her words carefully. "He belongs to someone else. Can you imagine how sad his real owner must be right now? It wouldn't be right to keep him."

Patty didn't want to hear the words her cousin was saying. Stubbornly Patty replied, "Maybe he doesn't have an owner. Maybe he's all alone, and that's why he jumped in our trunk. He wanted to be with us." Pausing she added, "Maybe I could keep him a secret? No one has to know. He's very smart. I can teach him to hide, and he can be really quiet when he wants to be. I think it could work. I'm sure it could!" Patty said these words with more confidence than she actually felt. Just as she was ready to add a few more convincing words, the bedroom door flew open and in walked Lori Lynn. The sudden addition of another body in the room caught Chatters completely off guard. With a loud screech and a big leap, Chatters headed for Patty's discarded backpack. The little monkey quickly disappeared. Lori Lynn looked down at the backpack in horror, and before Patty or Tosha could stop her, she ran from the room. They could both hear her screams all throughout the house as Lori headed straight for her mom.

"Mommy, Mommy! There's a wild animal in Patty's room, Mommy, Mommy!" Lori cried out as she entered the kitchen.

Patty froze in shock. She didn't know what to do. As she glanced over at Tosha for advice, she saw her cousin had that, *I told you so*, look on her face. "What?" Patty said, a little louder than she meant too.

"Looks to me like your secret just became public knowledge. I think *now* would be a good time to use that story we came up with earlier," Tosha said, trying to hide a smile.

The next thing Patty heard was her mom calling her. Now, normally Patty's mom was a very calm person. She hardly ever raised her voice and always allowed Patty the chance to explain things. This time however, her mom's voice had an undeniable tone of urgency to it.

Without delay, Patty snatched up her backpack and ran to the kitchen to face her mom. There was no point in putting off the inevitable. She had to try and make her mom understand that Chatters was a very good monkey and would make the perfect pet for the whole family. Halfway to the kitchen Patty almost crashed into her mom in the hallway.

"Patty, what in the world is your sister talking about? She says you have a wild animal in your room!"

"Well," Patty tried to explain, "that's not exactly right. I wouldn't call him a wild animal. He's actually very friendly," Patty said in a small voice. Her arms were wrapped protectively around her backpack.

Her mother wanted answers. She looked down at her daughter with a firm expression across her face. "Patty, what are you trying to say? Did you bring home a stray dog or cat? You know we agreed to wait a while before getting a pet." Patty's mother patiently explained the well-known agreement as she put her arm around her daughter and walked with her into the kitchen. Tosha followed at a distance, she wanted to stay as far out of this conversation as possible. Once Patty and her mom entered the kitchen, Lori Lynn ran to her mother's side. Lori's big blue eyes were glued to the backpack her sister was holding in her arms. Lori had seen the strange monkey climb in it, and wanted to stay close to her mother, just in case he was still in there.

Patty's mom gently put her hands on Patty's shoulders and sat her down in one of the kitchen chairs. Then she slowly pulled the backpack from Patty's arms, setting it on the table. Her mom sat down across the table from her daughter. The table had been cleared off in preparation for dinner later that day, with the exception of the customary bowl of fresh fruit in the center. It was obvious to Patty that her mom was waiting for an explanation, she just didn't know where to start. She sat at the table looking over at her backpack trying to remember the story she and Tosha were planning to use. She noticed the movement in her backpack and she feared what was coming. Within seconds, Chatters made his escape. He crawled out of the bag and with one tiny jump, sat right in the middle of the fruit bowl. Helping himself to a ripe yellow banana, he calmly looked around with what appeared to be a tiny smile upon his face. Patty's mom jumped up so fast that her chair fell over backwards and with a loud crash, hit the kitchen floor.

"Patty!" she exclaimed loudly. "What on earth is that?" Her mother hardly ever yelled, so this outburst caught Patty off-guard. She did not expect her mom to be afraid of something that Patty herself thought was so adorable. Patty tried unsuccessfully to suppress her giggles, she just couldn't imagine her mom being frightened by something as small as Chatters.

"Mom, it's okay. He's very friendly. See, he's smiling at you." Patty sputtered out the words while holding her hand over her mouth to hide her giggles.

Patty's mom generally loved animals, but she had never had a monkey in her house, or in her fruit bowl. "Patty, get him off the kitchen table right now!" She gestured with her hands for Patty to take action and to be quick about it. "Patty, we can't have a monkey in our house. Where did you get him?"

Things were not going as Patty had hoped. Lori Lynn had spoiled everything by walking into her room before she had the chance to figure out how to approach her mom with the whole monkey idea. Patty looked over at her cousin with a *now what* look in her eyes. Tosha coaxed her cousin with hand gestures to tell the story they had come up with. Cautiously, Patty began, "Well Mom, you see, we were walking back from Angelica's house and this little guy just ran out from nowhere and jumped in my backpack. We tried to get him out, but he wouldn't budge. We didn't see anyone around, so we just brought him home with us. I thought that maybe I could keep him. Please! I'll take care of him. You won't have to do anything with him. Really! Please?" Patty used her best pleading voice and the most adorable pout she could come up with.

"Patty," her mother paused and took a deep breath. She bent over and picked up the chair. "Monkeys are very expensive pets. Someone is probably looking for him right now. It's too late today, but first thing tomorrow morning you and Tosha go back to Angelica's and find out which of her neighbors has a missing monkey. It shouldn't be hard to find his owner. However, if you don't find them, we'll run an advertisement in the local paper. One way or another, you can't keep him. Do you understand?"

Patty's shoulders slumped and she very reluctantly nodded in acknowledgment of her mother's demands. Patty's mom watched as the two saddened girls walked slowly back to Patty's bedroom, the monkey cradled lovingly in her daughter's arms. Patty's mother felt terrible that her daughter had actually thought she could keep a monkey as a house pet. She always hated to disappoint either of her daughters, but this kind of pet was just not possible.

Once inside Patty's room, Tosha and Patty watched Chatters play. Big tears filled Patty's eyes. She rarely cried, but this disappointment was very hard to take. "Tosha, can't you come up with one of your brilliant ideas? There's got to be some way we can talk my mom into letting me keep him."

"Patty," Tosha said softly, "I tried to warn you. I didn't think your mom would like the idea of you having a monkey. He needs to be returned to his rightful owner." Patty wasn't ready to think about giving up Chatters. She just wanted to play with him and pretend he was hers, now and forever.

CHAPTER SIX

# THE MISSING DIARY

Tosha wore a thoughtful little frown, thinking about what tomorrow would bring. She knew the only way to get Chatters back to his owner was to go back and get in the trunk again. She was equally certain that if they read the same page of the diary, they would end up at the same place they had been earlier today. But were her suspicions correct about how the diary got them back? Tosha knew what to do. She reached for her backpack. It was time to find the answers to her questions. She unzipped the bag and plunged her hand deep inside it. Her fingers searched for the little box. A deep frown covered her face. Where was it? She couldn't feel it anywhere in her backpack. She grew worried.

Patty looked up and noticed her cousin tossing everything out of her backpack item by item. "What's wrong Tosha, what are you looking for?" Patty asked as she felt Chatters climb from one shoulder over to her other shoulder.

Tosha's face clouded with a look of pure panic. As she spoke, her voice conveyed her fears. "Patty, I can't find the diary, it's gone. Where could it be? Did you take it out of my backpack?"

"No, of course not," answered Patty. She watched as Tosha dumped her backpack completely upside down, and then shook it and pulled it inside out. There was no doubt that the diary was gone. Patty checked every pocket of Tosha's backpack while Tosha looked under Patty's bed, but still no diary. Then they searched Patty's backpack just to make sure. Before they were finished they had turned Patty's whole room upside down. Tosha was nearly sick with worry and disappointment.

"Are you sure you brought it? Maybe it's still at the mansion, or what if it fell out on the way home," Patty suggested.

"No Patty! I know I had it. You don't suppose that Lori Lynn found it while we were in the kitchen with your mom, do you? I can't remember if she was in there with us the whole time or not, can you?" Tosha was trying to think of any possible solution. She was so upset she just wanted to sit down and cry.

A small part of Patty couldn't help but feel relieved. If the diary was lost, then they couldn't return Chatters. Her mom could run all the ads she wanted to, no one would call because no one around here owned him. This way her mom would have to let her keep Chatters as her very own pet. Yet another part of her was looking forward to traveling in the trunk again. Just thinking of all the neat places they could go was very exciting.

Evening came and the girls got ready for bed, but sleep came very slowly for Tosha. Even after she drifted off, she tossed and turned all night. She had terrible dreams and was grateful to see the morning finally come.

Patty on the other hand had a wonderful night's rest. Her mother had allowed Chatters to stay in Patty's room for the night, however she had requested that Patty not let him sleep in her bed. So Patty came up with a brilliant idea, she made a bed on the floor for her and Chatters to sleep in. Once the bed was all arranged, she tucked him in with his own pillow and blanket. Then she snuggled down in the covers and slept like a baby. Her sleep was filled with dreams of traveling all over the world in the trunk, with Chatters by her side.

The morning light streamed into the bedroom, and Patty rolled over and squinted as it shined brightly in her eyes. She sat up and looked over to see the tiny monkey still sleeping soundly. She wanted to close the blinds and snuggle back down into the covers, but then noticed Tosha was already up and dressed. She was moving around the room, apparently still searching for the missing diary. "Tosha, you're already dressed. What time is it?"

Tosha was bent over in Patty's closet and she was digging around. She straightened up and glanced at her watch. "It's 7:40. Why don't you get up and help me. I can't give up, I have to find it." It was apparent that Tosha was frustrated, and it was putting her in a very bad mood.

"Tosha why don't we retrace our steps back to the mansion, we can look all around the area where we stopped and ate lunch yesterday. Maybe it slipped out then," Patty offered.

Tosha turned and looked at her cousin. "Patty, that's a great idea. I bet that's exactly what happened! Come on, get dressed. I want to go as soon as we can. Tosha noticed Chatters had crawled under his blanket and was bouncing up and down. It was a funny sight to see, and finally Tosha relaxed and allowed herself to giggle out loud.

Patty turned around and smiled, "So you finally decided to wake up." She joined her cousin's giggling while she gently tickled him through the blanket. Chatters's high- pitched noises filled her room. Patty got dressed and quickly folded up all the blankets she had spread out on her floor.

While Patty was getting dressed and folding the blankets, Tosha busied herself throwing everything back into her backpack that she had scattered all over the room.

They heard Patty's mom call them to breakfast. Patty slung her backpack over her shoulder and Chatters immediately jumped up and settled on top of it, ready for his free ride. Tosha looked over and saw him. Shaking her head back and forth, she was amazed at how comfortable he was with Patty. It was as if

Patty had been his owner forever. They both left the room and made their way down the hall.

After a big morning hug, Patty's mom started going over what the girls needed to do about the uninvited monkey. Patty listened and kept nodding her head up and down. "Yes, Mom, I know." Patty stretched her hand out to reach for the last banana from the fruit bowl. She handed it up to Chatters, who today remained on her backpack. He must have known the table was off-limits to him.

The girls had a quick breakfast, then away they went to fulfill Patty's mother's strict instructions to return the monkey. Neither cousin had a clue as to how they were going to manage that. Without the diary, there was no way.

They walked down the street both keeping their eyes on the ground, searching the pavement and the grassy area beside the road, nothing was said between them. Chatters did his best to cheer both of them up, but even Patty was quiet. After about fifteen minutes, they found themselves standing at the patio doors of Graybrook. Silently, they entered the house and headed straight for the stairs. They moved past the dark hallway and the tall suit of armor, around the corner and through the attic door, walking straight over to the trunk. The girls stood there quietly looking down at the trunk.

It was Chatters who finally broke the silence. He jumped off of Patty's shoulder and started dancing on the trunk lid. He jumped up and down, did back-flips, and bobbed his little head up and down, chattering the whole time. Then he put his tiny hands over his mouth as if he was trying to hold back his joy. He did this little dance over and over, until the girls started laughing and joined in the fun. They started out by laughing at him, and then Patty tried to imitate his dance, then Tosha did the same.

Dancing and laughing, the girls quickly forgot their worries. Tosha sat down on the floor and watched as Patty chased Chatters around the trunk. He ran up the side of it and tried to raise the lid to climb inside. Of course it was too heavy for him, so Patty assisted by opening the lid for him.

He immediately jumped inside and almost disappeared into the depths of it. Just about the time Patty started to bend down and pet him, he bounced up and perched on the edge of the trunk, holding something in his tiny hands. "Oh, my gosh! Tosha, look!" Patty squealed out. Tosha's eyes froze on Chatters and what he was now holding out to Patty. It was a small box.

Tosha jumped to her feet, she was afraid to get her hopes up. "Patty, it's the box the diary was in!" Tosha reached for it before Patty even had a chance to. Snatching the little box from Chatters's outstretched hands and taking a deep breath, she carefully opened the box. Slowly lifting the lid, Tosha peeked inside. To her total delight, it was there. The diary was there, just the way they found it yesterday when they first discovered it. Patty was just inches away and saw the beautiful red and gold book inside the box. She too was surprised and relieved that the diary was not lost, but kind of a little disappointed. She was still hoping to keep Chatters.

Tosha thought for a minute. She remembered reaching down and touching the outside of her backpack on their way home the day before, and she had felt the diary inside it. How did it end up back in the trunk? It was just one more of the magical mysteries surrounding the trunk and diary. For now, Tosha was just happy to have it back in her hands.

Chatters kept jumping in the trunk and back out again. He pulled on Patty's hand, and then repeated the process again and again. "Look," Patty said, "he acts like he wants us to get in the trunk." Without hesitation, Patty complied and climbed into the trunk with Chatters. Tosha got in right behind her cousin, and both girls made themselves comfortable. Tosha cast all doubts aside. Everything worked out just fine yesterday, why wouldn't it today? "The first thing we need to do is go back to the marketplace where we were yesterday. We can return Chatters to his rightful place, and this time, let's explore the market," Tosha said getting more excited by the second.

"I don't want to take him back yet. We can do that later. Let's look in the diary and see what other places there are that we could visit," Patty said in a convincing tone. She had lost all her fear and sense of caution.

Tosha didn't know if that was a good thing or not. She shot her cousin a warning glance. "Patty, we agreed to take him back. Your mom won't let you keep him anyway. He should be back where he belongs!" Tosha's tone was a little more scolding than she had meant it to be. "I'm sorry Patty, I know how much you like him, but it has to be done. Come on now. Here, you can read the diary this time. Find the place where we were yesterday, and let's see what happens."

Both girls reached up for the lid at the same time, and slowly brought it down. The semi-darkness closed in on them and then vanished as flashlights came on and lit up the inside. Patty didn't want to give up Chatters, but she knew Tosha was right. She opened the diary and began reading aloud.

*Her father had discovered one of the largest tombs ever found in this region. His daughter and her beloved pet were on-site to share in her father's discovery. There was much excitement at the camp today. Her father had been searching for something of this importance for years. There was bound to be great riches and endless historical items to retrieve and catalogue.*

"No Patty," Tosha said, stopping her cousin. "You're not reading the same page as yesterday. Give me the diary and let me see if I can find the right page!" Just as Tosha reached for the diary, Chatters slipped off of Patty's shoulder and fell into her lap. Patty dropped the diary and her flashlight, accidently bumping Tosha and knocking the flashlight out of her hand. Both girls scrambled to retrieve the book and find the flashlights. Patty couldn't see anything, and opened the trunk in an effort to get more light for their search.

# CHAPTER SEVEN

# EMMA

Neither of them were aware that they were no longer in the attic. They were focused on their search deep inside the trunk, until the sound of loud chattering filled their ears. Chatters jumped from Patty's lap, up to the edge of the trunk. One short leap took him to the ground outside and he scampered off. This brought Patty's head up with a snap. She wasn't shocked this time when she saw large tents and dirt streets. She was able to get one quick glimpse of Chatters just before he disappeared from sight. "Oh, no! Tosha look! There goes Chatters, he's running away! We have to go after him, come on!" Patty scrambled out of the trunk and started running after him.

Tosha straightened up just in time to see Patty running down a narrow dirt street. She reacted quickly, grabbing both backpacks and jumping out of the trunk. She chased after Patty at a hard run. Once she reached her, she tackled her to the ground to stop her.

"Tosha, let go of me! Chatters is going to get lost. I have to go after him!" Sobs were coming from Patty as she tried to free herself from her cousin's grip.

"Patty, I think you'd better look around before you go running off into the great unknown, because that's exactly where we are, the unknown. You were reading from a totally different part of the diary, and now here we are."

They looked around them, taking in their surroundings. Patty had been so intent on not losing sight of Chatters, she had not worried about where they were. It was dusk, and getting darker by the minute. They appeared to be in a camp of some sort with large white tents lining the road. To their left was a small marketplace, and just beyond that was an exotic-looking city, with large gold dome-shaped roofs.

"Tosha where are we, and why is it dark? It wasn't dark when we left home, it was early morning." Patty could feel the fear creeping back into her body. Her courage and desire for traveling in the trunk were quickly shrinking.

"I don't know where we are," Tosha said as she looked around. She fought to keep the concern that was growing quickly into fear out of her voice.

The girls were still sitting on the ground trying to decide what to do when they heard a strange voice from somewhere behind them. "Hello, are you two lost? Can I be of assistance?" Both Patty and Tosha jumped. Patty grabbed Tosha by her arm and held on tight. They scrambled to their feet as their eyes searched for the person speaking to them. A ghostly silhouette of billowing-white floated out of the shadows. Patty let out a small gasp. She couldn't believe her eyes. "Tosha," Patty whispered as she tugged on her cousin's arm. "It's the girl I saw in the marketplace yesterday!" Patty's eyes were large as she watched the girl come closer. She was wearing a white dress that swirled around her ankles as she walked toward them. Perched on her shoulder was the mischievous Chatters. When Patty spotted the monkey she jumped with glee, "Oh Chatters, there you are! I'm so happy to see you're alright."

The little girl looked at Patty and smiled, "Oh, so I have you to thank for returning my lost friend? Thank you very much. Oh my, where are my manners? Allow me to introduce myself, my name is Emma." The girl's voice was very soft and she had a strong accent. Patty and Tosha had never heard a voice as smooth and beautiful as Emma's. She fascinated them. Emma waited patiently for Patty to answer her question.

Tosha elbowed her cousin gently. "Oh, my name is Patty and this is my cousin Tosha. We're not from around here," Patty said with a friendly smile on her face. Emma looked at both girls warmly, taking in their appearance.

The cousins were wearing denim shorts and t-shirts with white tennis shoes and white socks. Emma raised one eyebrow and politely said, "Yes, I rather guessed that you weren't. Are you lost? Do you have a place to stay the night? My father and I have a lovely suite at the hotel." She gestured to the large building behind her, illuminated with many brightly lit windows. "Would you like to stay with us tonight?"

"Oh no," Patty said, "we have to get home. My mother would be worried sick if we were gone all night."

"Well then, would you at least accept my invitation to dinner? Please say yes. We've been away from home for over a year now. I miss all of my friends, and there is no one my age I can talk to. You simply must say yes!" Emma exclaimed, her accent making the invitation sound almost dramatic.

Through all this exchange of conversation, Tosha's mind was working fast. She studied the girl standing in front of them. One thing in particular caught her eye. Tosha loved jewelry and was always admiring other people's earrings and bracelets. It was Emma's necklace that now held Tosha's full attention. The chain was made of braided gold and silver. Dangling from it was a charm in the shape of a teardrop. The teardrop must have been hollow because there was something in it that bounced around each time Emma moved. It was the most elegant necklace she had ever laid eyes on.

Emma's clothes were also unlike anything Tosha had seen before. She wore a pair of short white gloves that were made of lace. Her dress looked like something a movie star would wear, even her shoes were fancy. They were also white, and had a little bit of a heel. Tosha had begged her mom for a pair of high-heeled shoes, but her mother had refused, saying she was too young for shoes like that. Each item Emma was wearing matched perfectly. Tosha estimated her age to be about ten, maybe a little older. Everything about her seemed so grown up, so elegant, and so different from anyone Tosha had ever known. Tosha wanted the chance to get to know her better. She imagined what it would be like to stay with Emma overnight, or even just for dinner. What a fantastic experience this could be. She and Patty would have so much fun if they could just stay for a little while. And if her theory was right about time standing still while they were gone, how could they refuse?

Tosha nudged her cousin in the side. They looked at each other and both silently agreed. "Yes, we'd be honored to have dinner with you and your father," Tosha said in a cheerful voice. Both girls were very happy about going to the hotel with Emma, Tosha was almost skipping she was so excited. This was surely a dream. Yes, a dream come true.

# CHAPTER EIGHT

# DINNER IN THE BALLROOM

They walked the short distance to the hotel. When they turned and started up the long steps of the massive structure, Patty's joy began to fade. Everywhere she looked, she saw elegantly dressed people, and many of them spoke a strange language. It was like they were in an entirely different world, not just a different country. She felt so out of place. There was no way they could go to dinner with Emma and her father dressed in shorts and t-shirts. Patty slowed her pace, and Tosha could tell something was bothering her. "Come on Patty, let's go," Tosha coaxed as she tugged on her cousin's hand.

Tosha was practically dragging Patty by the time they reached the big doors of the hotel. "Wait Tosha," Patty protested. "We can't go in there looking like this!" Patty exclaimed, looking down at her clothes. "Just look at us! We'll embarrass Emma and her father, not to mention ourselves!"

Tosha stopped and gazed down at her own shorts and t-shirt. Then she peered over her shoulder at the people walking here and there, near the front of the hotel. "Patty, look around you," Tosha said in a low voice. "Do you see anyone staring at us? Do you see anyone even looking at us?"

Patty's eyes searched the crowd. Tosha was right, not one person was looking at either of them. It was amazing. No one was paying any attention to them at all. Wow, Patty thought, I wonder if anyone else can see us? Leaning over, Patty got close to her cousin's ear and whispered, "Tosha, do you think we're invisible?"

"I don't know, but it doesn't matter," Tosha said, without a care. She was too excited to worry about their clothing choice of the day. "Now come on, Emma is waiting for us!"

Patty took a deep breath and, hand-in-hand, the two girls followed Emma into the big hotel. They were overwhelmed by the grandness of it all. There were huge chandeliers hanging from high ceilings. Every wall displayed long mirrors with ornate, gold frames. The entire ceiling was painted with clouds and angels with little white doves scattered about. Everywhere they looked they saw large golden cages with live parrots of assorted colors. Their loud whistles could be heard above the many voices in the lobby. Tosha had never seen any place so elegant or so grand. They followed Emma through the lobby and up the stairs to the family suite. When Emma opened the door, Patty and Tosha were overwhelmed.

Patty's jaw dropped open. Finding her voice she said, "I didn't know that they made hotel rooms this big." She blinked, thinking she was surely imagining all this.

Chatters climbed from Emma's shoulder down into her arms. He seemed very happy to be back with Emma. Emma smiled down at him and then she turned back to her guests saying, "This suite has four bedrooms, two bathing rooms, a parlor and a study." Patty and Tosha followed Emma as she led the way to her bedroom. Once inside, Emma gently closed the door. She then proceeded straight to the far side of the room and disappeared behind a strange looking partition.

"Patty," Tosha said nudging her cousin. "That's what they call a dressing screen. I've read about them. People used them to dress behind, you know for privacy," Tosha said. The girls were entertained by Chatters while they waited for her to return. He had jumped up onto the bed and was bouncing up and down, having a great time.

After about five minutes Emma came back with her arms full of dresses, slips, gloves and other accessories. She laid these items out on her bed and turned to address the two cousins. Patty and Tosha stood watching her, their eyes full of wonder. Emma looked up at them and said, "I thought you might want to dress, before you meet my father. Dinner will be in an hour. I'm supposed to meet him downstairs in the formal dining room. Do you think that will be enough time for you both to change?" Emma questioned politely, as she again walked behind the screen. Chatters started trying to pull one of the gloves over his head.

Tosha was the first of the cousins to find her voice. "You mean you want us to wear these. I mean…you don't mind if we wear your…your clothes?"

Patty stood by the bed looking down at the array of beautiful dresses, her fingers just itching to try them on. "We get to wear these to dinner? How wonderful!" Patty squealed in delight.

Tosha moved over by the bed to join her. Both girls grinned ear to ear as they started picking up one item after another, they hardly knew where to start. Emma returned again and this time she was loaded down with assorted shoes, handbags and hats. With her ever-present friendly smile, she laid these items down beside the dresses and looked over at Tosha. "Well," she said, "we're all about the same size, and I have plenty enough to share."

"Wonderful," Patty said, jumping with joy. She shot Tosha a look of total delight. Tosha couldn't resist reaching over and giving Emma a big hug. "Thank you, Emma, we'd love to dress for dinner." Emma pointed over toward the dressing screen, "If you like, you may use this to dress behind."

They thanked Emma again. They were in heaven trying on one dress and then another, until at last they both found the perfect fit and style. While they were changing, they all talked non-stop. Emma stood on the other side of the dressing screen enjoying the conversation. She helped them with the stockings and shoes. It was a good thing too, because the shoes had lots of tiny little buttons on them. They were impossible for Patty or Tosha to manage alone. Emma used a special little tool to pull each button through the buttonhole on the shoes.

Once they were finished, they grabbed their shorts and t-shirts and shoved them into their backpacks. Tosha walked over and stood beside Emma, looking into the mirror. She couldn't take her eyes off of Emma's necklace. Standing this close to her, Tosha could see the tiny star that was encased inside the tear-drop pendant, it seemed to sparkle just like a real star. "Emma," Tosha said, "I have to ask you something, I hope you don't think I'm being rude. Your necklace, it's so unusual. It's the most beautiful thing I've ever seen. Where did you get it"?

Emma's hand moved to the necklace and her fingers gently caressed the elegant teardrop. A sadness filled Emma's eyes, and Tosha instantly regretted mentioning it.

"Oh no," she replied graciously, "you're not being rude at all. This belonged to my mother. She died when I was born. This necklace was her favorite piece of jewelry. We have a beautiful portrait of her wearing this very necklace in our parlor at home."

Tosha was sorry the subject had caused her new friend a painful memory. "Gosh, I'm sorry Emma, I didn't know. It must be awful not having a mom?"

"Yes, it is at times," Emma said with a hint of sadness in her voice. "But my father tries very hard to be both mother and father to me, and he hardly ever leaves me behind on his many trips. Even though I get homesick, I would far rather be here with him than at home without him. I have truly enjoyed all the places I've traveled with my father, and Chatters keeps me company when father is working. I just miss having someone my own age to be with, to talk to. That's why I'm so pleased you two accepted my dinner invitation, I'm certain we're going to have a lovely evening."

When they were ready to go downstairs, Emma brought them each a string of pearls to wear. The girls walked over to the mirror and admired themselves. They were amazed by their reflections. They looked so grown up. "My mother would flip if she saw me like this," Patty said, wearing a big grin.

"Yeah," Tosha agreed, "yours and mine both. I've never worn anything so beautiful. I feel like Cinderella! I wonder if we're going to turn into pumpkins at midnight!" Patty and Tosha looked at each other and started giggling.

"Well, if you are both ready, I think we had better be going down to dinner now," Emma said as she walked over to Chatters and scooped him up. "Good night Chatters," she said as she placed him in his cage. "We'll be back soon." She gave him a pat on his head and walked over to Patty and Tosha. "Ready?" she asked with a sweet smile on her face.

The two cousins took one last glance in the mirror, looked at Emma and nodded. Just before walking out into the hallway, Tosha turned to Emma and gave her another hug. "Thank you so much."

"Me too," Patty followed Tosha's example and threw her arms around Emma, hugging her tightly. "I was so worried about looking out of place. Now I can go to dinner and enjoy myself, thank you!" Patty said, smiling brightly at Emma.

"It's my pleasure Patty, it was nothing really."

Patty and Tosha were now eager to meet Emma's father. All three girls made their way down the stairs towards the dining room, with Emma leading the way. As they walked through the lobby, Emma told them that many years ago this hotel had been a palace and that royalty had lived here. In fact, the formal dining room they were having dinner in used to be a ballroom. Patty and Tosha were both fascinated by this, imagining what it must have looked like filled with royalty.

The three girls entered the dining room and paused as Emma searched for her father. From across the room, a tall gentleman stood and walked toward them. Emma proudly introduced her two new friends to him. "Father, I'd like to introduce you to Miss Tosha, and her cousin, Miss Patty. They have been kind enough to accept my invitation to join us for dinner tonight." Emma's father gave a low bow to the girls, and to Tosha's surprise, he kissed the back of her hand, and then did the same to Patty's.

Both girls were mesmerized as they watched every move he made. As he straightened up, he gave them a warm smile, and they smiled right back. He was very tall and slender. His hair was jet black and parted straight down the middle with both sides combed back and slicked down. He had the biggest mustache either of them had ever seen. His smile, just like Emma's, was contagious as he acknowledged each girl. Then, very formally, he offered his arm to his daughter. Emma reached her hand out, and placing it on her father's arm, they regally walked to the table.

Tosha couldn't resist. She offered her arm to Patty who gracefully placed her hand on Tosha's arm, and they followed the father and daughter to their table. It was a struggle for Patty to hold in her giggles. Tosha, on the other hand, was nearly overwhelmed by the grandness of it all. She didn't know what to do first, laugh or cry. She felt like the luckiest girl alive to be at such a beautiful place, and wearing such a gorgeous dress. She wondered if she should pinch herself to make sure she wasn't dreaming.

During the meal, the two cousins carefully observed Emma and did just as she did. They were a little nervous. There were six pieces of silverware, three plates, a formal napkin, and two goblets at each place-setting. They did not want to embarrass themselves, Emma or her father. Patty and Tosha watched Emma and her father in awe. Emma's father was so distinguished looking and Emma was so beautiful. Tosha again found herself gazing at the chain and pendant Emma wore around her neck. It reminded her of something a princess would wear, and Emma was the perfect princess.

They all four visited and slowly worked their way through each course of the meal. It was nothing like dinner time at home, Tosha thought. This meal was more of an event to be savored and enjoyed, and that's exactly what they were doing.

The entire evening was like being in a fairy tale, but like all fairy tales, the girls knew this delightful adventure must soon come to an end. Dinner was nearly over and Tosha did not want it to be. Her thoughts were forcing her to return to reality and she began to worry about how they would get back home. Taking a deep breath, she scolded herself; don't think about it now, not now!

When they were all finished, Emma's father excused himself and joined some other gentlemen who were sitting at a nearby table. Emma stood up. Patty and Tosha followed her lead and the three of them filed out of the dining room, back through the awe-inspiring lobby to the staircase, and back to Emma's room.

CHAPTER NINE

# EXPLORING THE TOMB

Patty and Emma walked over to Chatters's cage and Patty opened his door. He was obviously happy to see them both and jumped back and forth from Patty to Emma. He clapped his tiny hands together and shrieked loudly. While the other two girls laughed at the funny monkey, Tosha wandered over and sat on a small sofa located near the dressing screen. She reached for the tool Emma had used earlier and worked to unbutton her shoes, absentmindedly thinking that her mom was right, she wasn't ready for high heels yet. They were pretty, but not very comfortable.

She watched Emma and Patty play with Chatters while her mind wondered about how hard it was going to be to find the trunk. Once they found it, she hoped she could get the diary to cooperate and get them back home. She was *fairly* certain that all she needed to do was re-read the same page she had read earlier. Yes, that should do it. She twisted her hands together, what if it didn't work? A sudden shudder traveled down her back and she shook all over. Everything will be all right, everything will be all right, Tosha kept repeating to herself. It just had to be! Tosha took a deep breath, she wasn't going to worry about it anymore right now. They would be leaving soon enough, no need to worry just yet. She got up and walked over to Emma's bed where the other two girls had made themselves comfortable.

They talked about all sorts of things, but the most interesting was the worldly experiences Emma had to share. She had traveled to many countries, some very different, and others not so different than America. She talked to the girls about some of the most unusual things she had seen. They loved listening to her. Patty slid off the bed and walked over to Emma's bedroom window. She craned her neck to look down at the busy street in front of the hotel. It was a little hard to see because of the balcony just outside the window.

Emma and Tosha moved off the bed and over to where Patty was standing. "What's so interesting Patty?" Tosha asked.

"Oh, I was just watching all the people on the street. Emma, can we go out onto your balcony?" Patty asked, pointing out the window. We could see everything much better from out there."

"Oh, that's not a balcony, that's the fire escape. All big hotels have them," she replied as she unlocked the window and pulled it up high so they could get a closer look at it. They all stuck their heads out the window and then, one by one, they climbed out onto it. Emma pointed out different places that were visible from the fire escape. She proudly pointed toward the camp site at the edge of the city. It was only a couple blocks from the hotel. As she pointed at it, she started telling the cousins about it.

"It's the largest tomb ever discovered in this part of the world, and my father believes it to be the tomb of a child emperor. When something like this is found, there is a lot of preparatory work to be done before they can actually start exploring it. Generally, my father allows me to go with him into his digs once they have the site prepared. I have not been in this one yet, but my father said I could come with him one day next week and explore whatever part of it I wanted to."

"Wow," Tosha said, "I think that would be the coolest thing ever, to be able to explore something that old."

"Me too," Patty replied wishfully.

Emma grabbed Tosha's hand. "Tosha, Patty," she said sounding excited, "I have a dreadfully naughty thought. Would you both like to go down into the dig? My father will be playing cards until the wee hours of the morning. We should have plenty of time."

"Oh yes, could we?" Tosha answered, letting all her worries of how to return home fade away. Patty was right next to her cousin, nodding her head up and down vigorously.

"All right then, we'll need to change our clothes and I'll get my knap-sack," Emma said as she climbed back into the room and disappeared behind her dressing screen. She knew her father would disapprove of her going into any dig without him. She wasn't in the habit of going behind her father's back, but she considered herself to be quite a brave and capable young lady. She was confident that the dig was safe. After all, workers had been preparing it for weeks now.

The girls all busied themselves changing their clothes; Emma into her special gear and the cousins changed back into their shorts and t-shirts. Tosha smiled as she slipped back into her comfortable tennis shoes, allowing a soft sigh to escape her lips.

When Emma stepped out from behind the dressing screen, Patty had to suppress an overwhelming desire to laugh. She stood there in front of them wearing so much gear that she looked like a miniature *Indiana Jones,* right down to the hat. Her outfit included khaki knee-pants and tall socks that matched. She also wore a wide belt around her waist with assorted items hanging from it, but the only thing Patty could identify was a thick mass of rope. Emma looked completely prepared.

"Is everyone ready?" Emma asked as she walked over and picked up Chatters and once again placed him inside his cage.

She knew there was no way they could take the little monkey where they were going.

The cousins grabbed their backpacks, waiting for Emma to lead the way. They were surprised when she walked over to her bedroom window and stepped out onto the fire escape again. Emma looked back through the open window and said, "This way ladies. My father would lock me up for a month if he saw us walk through the lobby of the hotel, on our way to his dig. He is rather protective of me and doesn't think I can take care of myself. Even though I am a lady, he has taught me well, and I can manage a dig better than most men I've observed."

The girls walked over and joined Emma on the fire escape. She instructed them to follow her, single file, and to be careful. The fire escape was a new adventure in itself. It consisted of many short sets of steps. They watched as Emma pressed down hard on each set as she came to them. One by one, they descended cautiously until they came to the next set. Patty didn't like them at all, they felt wobbly and she feared they would fall apart under the girls' weight. It was a new experience for the girls, but they all managed it with no accidents. Once on solid ground, they walked the short distance to the dig site.

On the way, Emma started explaining to the girls what to expect once they got to the dig. "We'll have to climb down a ladder. All you have to do is take your time and don't look down. It always looks much deeper than it really is, so I have learned to simply, *not look*. Once we get to the bottom, we'll be looking for the reinforced tunnels that the workers have built. These types of tombs have several chambers, many of which are fake and hold nothing of real value. The one I think we would all enjoy exploring the most is the one my father told me about. It's the chamber that holds all the young emperor's personal items."

Patty and Tosha could not believe they were about to do something like explore the tomb of a child emperor, it all seemed so unreal. Even though they were excited beyond belief they remained silent, listening to everything Emma was telling them.

All three girls had stopped and were standing at the edge of the camp. Tosha was asking Emma a question about something, while Patty allowed her eyes to wander. Located just behind where they were standing, she saw a long row of large white tents that lined the camp site. There were a number of torches scattered about the camp, providing some light. She heard a noise. Turning in that direction, she saw a group of horses tied up just a few feet away from where they stood. "Oh look Tosha, there's a bunch of horses. Let's go pet them."

Emma quickly stepped in front of Patty to block her path. "Patty, those are not horses, they are mules. Mules can be very nasty, it's best we don't bother them." She gently reached out and took Patty by the hand, guiding her back toward the opening of the dig.

"Mules," Patty said with a curious frown on her face. "What good are mules? You can't even ride a mule, can you?"

"No Patty, not really," Emma responded. "The workers use them to haul artifacts up out of the dig. They are very strong, hard workers, and are extremely valuable to accomplish the work we do here." Emma stopped and looked down into a very large black hole in the ground.

Tosha and Patty joined her. Standing next to Emma the three peered down into the darkness, but all they could see was a large ladder sticking out of the hole about two feet. Attached to a post, near the entrance of the dig, was a strong thick rope. That rope traveled over to the hole and down along the side of the ladder. Tosha was the first to find the courage to ask the question that was on both their minds. "How far down is it, Emma?"

"Oh, my father estimates it to be over thirty feet. It took forty workers over six months to dig it, and another nine months to clear out and reinforce the tunnels they have prepared thus far. My father and I have visited this site many times to oversee the progress. Two weeks ago, we settled into the hotel and we will stay here until all the artifacts have been recovered."

It was clear to both of the cousins that Emma knew a lot about exploring underground tombs like this one. She seemed to know all about how everything was done. However, all this did little to settle the queasy feeling Patty felt creeping into the pit of her stomach. With some hesitation, Patty said, "It is so dark, I can't see the bottom." Patty looked from Tosha to Emma, her large eyes shining from the reflection of the torches. She was trying to imagine what it would be like to climb down a thirty-foot ladder in the dark.

Tosha was worried that Patty would lose her nerve, and not go down into the tomb. Before Emma had a chance to reply to Patty's statement, Tosha stepped over and wrapped her arm around her cousin. "Patty, don't worry, we have our flashlights. We can use them once we get down the ladder." Tosha gave Patty a tight squeeze and a pleading look to let her cousin know it was something she really wanted to do.

Patty understood the silent message Tosha was sending her. "Okay, okay, that's a good idea." Patty said softly. She really wanted to do this just as much as her eager cousin did, but it was hard for her to hold in the fear that was trying to take over. She could feel it. It was like ants crawling all over her arms and legs. She shivered and took a deep breath. Scolding herself, she kept repeating silently, I can do this…I can do this.

Emma had been listening to the cousins' conversation. Not sure what they were talking about, her curiosity got the best of her and she asked, "What are flashlights, I've never seen one?"

Immediately, Tosha dug down deep into her backpack and pulled out two small flashlights. She handed one to Emma and then held up the other one and snapped it on. A bright steady stream of light stretched out in front of them.

"Oh my goodness gracious! This is remarkable, a fire torch in a tiny cylinder." Emma held the flashlight up that Tosha had given her turning it over and over in her hand. She examined every inch of the small device. Then, locating the switch, she turned it on. Emma was delighted. Her face lit up even more brightly than the flashlight did. Tosha and Patty both giggled at the sight. Patty was relieved to have something to distract her from her worries, and Tosha was thrilled to have pleased her new friend. "You can keep it, I always carry a second one. You just never know when you'll need a little extra light," Tosha said, smiling happily.

"Oh, thank you, Tosha. I love it! It's wonderful!" Emma giggled along with the girls and everyone relaxed a little. She reached out and gave Tosha a big hug. "This is the most wonderful gift I have ever received. I will treasure it always," Emma said as she switched it off and tucked it into her knapsack. "We'll need both our hands free while climbing down the ladder," she explained to them.

Tosha took a deep breath and followed Emma's example, tucking her flashlight safely inside her backpack. The girls listened intently while Emma explained to them the best way to descend the long ladder. She told them that they each needed to stay about six-feet apart to give each other plenty of room on the ladder. "If you're both ready, I'll lead the way. Once we get near the bottom you'll know, because there should be several torches lit." With that said, Emma stepped over onto the ladder and started climbing down.

Patty reached out, and grabbing Tosha whispered, "I can't believe we're doing this, can you?" Her voice was shaking just a little.

"No, I feel like we're having the most incredible dream ever! You go next Patty, I'll go last okay?"

Patty nodded her head up and down, but she felt like her whole body was trembling uncontrollably, and she couldn't make it stop. She reached out a shaking hand and gripped the ladder. Her head was still nodding.

Per Emma's instructions, Patty tried not to look down. In fact, she didn't want to look at anything and that wasn't too hard, because it was too dark to see any of her surroundings.

After she climbed a short distance down into the hole, she was enveloped by a blackness so dense that she couldn't even see the ladder anymore. All she could do was feel her way. It was terrifying! She forced herself to keep moving downward. One step at a time, she slowly allowed her toes to search around for the next rung on the ladder. Each time, she made sure her foot was in place before she moved her other foot to repeat the process. She never took her hands off the ladder, but simply loosened them enough to slide them down as she moved deeper into the dig.

Tosha followed Patty onto the ladder, allowing her the six-feet or so spacing, as Emma had instructed them to do. She had only descended three or four steps when she noticed rather grotesque looking roots sticking out from the dirt walls that surrounded her. She imagined she could see something crawling around one of the larger roots. She squeezed her eyes shut, certain that it was a snake. Tosha had never done anything like this before. She knew that Patty had been involved in doing volunteer work with the youth group at her church. She had worked on projects where they painted houses, and raked yards for senior citizens. Tosha's community service had consisted of things like helping at Bible school, or working in the nursery. She had absolutely no experience with ladders, so she felt certain that Patty was handling this far better than she was. Talking to Emma helped distract Tosha from her fear of navigating down each step. She was equally certain that it was a good thing it was dark, because she was sure if she could see how far down thirty-feet actually looked, she would lose her nerve and she didn't want to miss out on the adventure of a lifetime.

Tosha and Emma talked back and forth some, but not Patty. She remained silent and focused on what her feet were doing. She even had to think about breathing. Everything in her life had slowed down to a crawl. She had no idea how much time had passed from when she first stepped onto the ladder, but she was thrilled when she finally heard Emma call out to them that she could see the light from the torches, indicating that they were near the bottom. She wanted to scream out with joy, but didn't dare break her concentration.

Emma jumped off the ladder and placed a supporting hand gently on Patty to let her know she was safe and sound, and at the bottom. Patty instantly relaxed, and stepping off the ladder, realized she had closed her eyes the whole way down. Opening them, she was happy to see that there were, indeed, several torches burning brightly. She stepped out of the way to make room for her cousin. All three girls hugged each other tightly for a few moments, very happy to be on firm ground.

Looking around them, Tosha and Patty were disappointed at first. They didn't know what to expect but they didn't think it would be more dirt walls. "Are we in the tomb? I thought the walls would be made of stone." Tosha hung her head, allowing her lack of enthusiasm to show.

"No, we are not in the tomb yet. This is a loading area. It gives the workers the room they need to attach artifacts to a rope so they can be pulled up and hauled away. I have not had the opportunity to explore this dig yet, but my father has told me all about the different chambers they have found." Emma turned and pointed over to an opening that was well-lit by a torch. "That's the way we need to go, over there."

The three girls walked over to it. "If I'm correct, we'll travel down this tunnel approximately twenty feet and we will then turn to our right. That will lead us to the chamber I want to explore. It should be the one that holds the young emperor's treasured belongings."

Tosha and Patty were excited, they had let go of their earlier fears now that they were off the ladder. Neither one of them wanted to think about the dreaded reality that the only way out, was to climb back up.

They followed Emma over to the opening. Emma stopped and reached for the oil torch that was on the wall next to the entrance. Suddenly she stopped and smiled, pulled her hand away, and reached into her knapsack. Pulling out her new gift, she switched on the flashlight. Patty and Tosha did the same and they all headed down the long tunnel. They came to the turn and went around the corner. Emma led them to another opening, but this one was different. It was like a real doorway, with large square stones across the top of the entrance. Emma pointed to the side and indicated to them a strange hook-like object that jutted out from the wall. "There used to be a door here, you see. This is what door hinges looked like, centuries ago," she said, pointing at it.

Stepping through the doorway was like walking into a whole different world. They all stopped and directed their flashlights here and there. Emma stepped over to a wall and pointed her flashlight towards where a torch hung on the wall. She reached into her knapsack and found some matches. She struck one and when it sparked, she touched it to the torch, instantly bathing the entire chamber in bright light. Patty and Tosha sucked in a deep breath of air as they gasped out loud at the beauty that surrounded them. Emma had seen many chambers before, but none as beautiful as this. She was equally as pleased as Patty and Tosha were.

"Wow," Patty exclaimed, "this is the most awesome thing I have ever seen." She switched off her flashlight and dropped it into her backpack, hurrying over to an open trunk in the corner of the chamber.

"Now, this is more like it," Tosha squealed. "It's more like being in a castle than a tomb." She walked over to where a massive hand-carved bed stood. The bed had a thick wooden headboard and footboard. The entire surface of each was carved into a city, with buildings and pathways. There was even a carving of horses pulling a cart. So much detail, that Tosha could envision what the city must have looked like long ago.

Emma was walking all around the room, examining one thing and then another. All the girls found numerous items of interest, but it was Emma who found the hidden treasure room.

"I found it," she announced loudly. "Come over here and help me move this trunk," she cried out with urgency in her voice.

Neither cousin had ever heard her call out so loudly. Her voice echoed off the walls. Tosha and Patty ran over to join her on the other side of the room. "What did you find, Emma?" Tosha asked, eagerly looking over Emma's shoulder. Patty was right beside her cousin, looking at the wall where Emma was pointing. There was a big trunk and she was pointing at something behind it.

"Please help me push this heavy trunk out of the way!" Emma was clearly excited about something. All three girls got on one end of it and shoved with all their strength. Finally, after several futile attempts, it started to move and once it did they kept at it until it was out of the way. Emma jumped around the trunk and pointed again toward the part of the wall that had been behind the trunk.

The girls saw that there was a large piece of cloth attached to the wall. As the girls watched, Emma pulled the cloth back and exposed a small opening in the wall. Tosha and Patty were stunned. Patty asked Emma what it was. Emma turned to them and explained. "This is a sub-chamber. It's a place where very important, valuable items or personal treasures are kept. They are always hidden behind something, and this one was behind that trunk. This is what I was hoping we would find." Without any further explanation, Emma switched on her flashlight and, getting down on her hands and knees, she crawled through the opening.

"Oh my gosh, she is fearless! She kind of reminds me of you, Tosha," Patty said smiling over at her cousin. They could hear Emma calling for them to follow her. "Ready or not, here we come," Patty replied. As she bent down and started to crawl into the sub-chamber, she realized she couldn't fit into the small opening wearing her backpack. She backed up, took it off, and after grabbing her flashlight, pushed the backpack aside. Keeping the flashlight in one hand, she crawled through the tiny opening and joined Emma.     Tosha observed what her cousin did, and followed.

Once the three of them were back together, they quickly realized just how small the treasure chamber was. It wasn't even high enough to stand up in. That didn't bother Emma or Tosha, they held onto their flashlights and crawled from item to item. Patty had never liked tight places. She worked to keep her panic under control, taking deep breaths and telling herself over and over that they wouldn't be in here for very long, not very long at all. She settled herself down right next to the opening and waited for the other girls to finish their detective work.

She had her flashlight on and shined it to the right and then to the left side of her. That's when she noticed a small wooden chest. It wasn't fancy like so many of the other boxes she had looked through in the room they had just come from. She scooted over a few inches to get closer to it. Laying her flashlight down beside it, she used both her hands to open the lid. There was just enough light to see inside. The chest was full of strange glass balls, which Patty assumed were marbles. They were bigger than the ones she used to play with, and were definitely different. Inside of each clear glass ball was a second, smaller ball of color. Each one appeared to be a different color. She picked up her flashlight and shined it down into the chest. When she did that, everything in the room changed.

A kaleidoscope of fiery color seemed to burst from the little chest. The light was so intense, she felt she needed to shield her eyes from the brightness. Instinctively, she pulled the flashlight away, but somehow they held onto their brilliance. It was as if the light from her flashlight, had energized them somehow. It was thrilling, and she couldn't resist the urge to reach her hand down inside the box and scoop up a handful of them to examine more closely. Snapping off her flashlight and slipping it into her pocket, she dipped her hands down into the chest. She loved the cool way the marbles felt when she touched them.

Tosha and Emma had noticed the colorful glow as it filled the small room. They crawled over and sat next to Patty, pure astonishment covering their faces. "Glory to goose bumps," Emma breathed. "I've never seen anything like this before."

# CHAPTER TEN

# THE DESPERATE ESCAPE

Just about the time Emma leaned over to pick up one of the amazing little balls, a tremor from deep underground shook the world around them. Panic filled their hearts. Emma headed straight for the tiny entryway and commanded them to follow her. She crawled out of the tiny treasure chamber and scrambled to her feet. She headed for the doorway that led out of the chamber. The whole time she kept looking behind her, checking on the other two, urgently shouting instructions at them. "Don't stop, you must keep up with me. We mustn't get trapped down here. When we get to the ladder, climb it as fast as you can. There is a rope attached to it, you can use it to hold onto as you climb up."

There was no time to think. All Tosha or Patty could do was to follow Emma as quickly as they could, and listen to everything she was telling them to do. Again, the ground shook and all three of them fell to their knees. A half-second later they were up and running again. Dust and dirt tumbled down into their eyes, their hair, and even into their mouths, coughing and choking them as they kept running. When they realized they had reached the loading area, a momentary feeling of relief flooded over them, but that didn't last long. Once again, the ground trembled and they teetered back and forth. Emma grabbed hold of the ladder, quickly explaining that she needed to go first. She knew she could climb faster and she knew where to get help if they needed it. No one disagreed with her decision. They clambered onto the ladder in the same order as they came down it; first Emma, then Patty, and last was Tosha.

If Patty thought the climb down was hard, there was no comparison to the difficult job it was to hold onto the ladder while it was moving violently, much less climb up it. It jerked and bounced continuously. Patty wasn't sure if they themselves were causing it on their speedy climb up the ladder, or if it was the unstable ground beneath them. Either way, it was horrifying.

Tosha couldn't believe that their awesome adventure was ending this way. Why did this have to happen? What if they got hurt and couldn't get home, or even worse, they could die. No one would ever know what happened to them. They would be considered missing children. This was all her fault. Patty was right after all, they should have left it alone. Right then and there Tosha made a decision, she would see to it that Patty got back home safe and sound. She closed the gap, catching up to Patty on the ladder. She yelled up to her cousin telling her she was right behind her, that she would keep her safe and that somehow, everything was going to be all right.

Patty's ears were ringing, she swore she could hear her own heart beating in them. She was having trouble keeping a good grip on the ladder. She couldn't imagine how Emma thought they could hold the rope and the ladder at the same time. Patty could hear her cousin trying to reassure her. She knew Tosha was worried. Suddenly, Patty realized she was still holding onto one of the marbles from the little box. How had she managed that? It glowed out at her and as her eyes focused on it, she could feel herself calming down. It even seemed easier to climb the unsteady ladder.

Tosha could see the dirt walls and realized they were nearing the top. She called reassurance up to Patty, figuring her cousin probably had her eyes closed. Then, something tragic happened. Another big tremor began building from below, and the ladder started to give way and break into pieces. Tosha yelled for her cousin to grab the rope. Patty heard Tosha's command and she grabbed hold of it. Unfortunately, Tosha was too close to Patty on the ladder, so that when Tosha reached for the rope, Patty's feet were in her way and she couldn't get a grip on it. Tosha felt herself falling with the ladder and her screams filled the tunnel.

At the same time all of this was happening, Patty faintly heard Emma calling down to them, "I'm at the top, hold on!" Patty heard her cousin's screams and she looked down, just in time to see her still clutching the ladder as it broke away with a loud cracking sound and smashed into the dirt wall. As Patty watched in horror, Tosha disappeared into the darkness below. Screaming loudly, Patty called down to her cousin, but the only sound that she heard was the ladder smashing to the floor of the dig. Patty's heart sank, and she cried out again. "Tosha, Tosha! Please answer me!" Patty gripped the rope even tighter. Sobs burst from her throat, she was crying so hard the sounds echoed off the dirt walls. Then, she thought she heard something. Suppressing her sobs and holding her breath, she listened. Relief flooded over her when she heard a muffled voice from somewhere below call out, "I'm okay, I'm okay." Tosha was trembling as she forced the words up to her cousin. "I've grabbed a root or something and I'm hanging on but I can't see you. I don't know how far I've fallen," Tosha choked out her words. The crash into the wall had nearly knocked the breath out of her.

"Oh my gosh! Thank goodness you're okay!" Patty's voice was a high-pitched shriek, but her relief was enormous. Patty looked up above her and could see Emma bending over the opening. Emma called down to Patty again, "I'm going to lower my rope down to you. I need each of you to tie it around your waist and I will pull you up." Emma tied her end of the rope to the same post the ladder rope was tied to, and then lowered it down to Patty. Then she vanished.

Patty didn't have the chance to tell Emma what had happened to Tosha. Looking back down into the darkness, Patty shouted to Tosha that help was coming and to hold on. Patty couldn't explain her calmness or the strength she seemed to have. It wasn't hard for her to hold onto the rope anymore or to grab the other rope Emma sent down to her. She did as Emma instructed and tied the rope around her waist. Looking down, she lowered the remainder of the rope, silently praying it was long enough for her cousin to grasp it. "Tosha, Emma wants us to use her rope. You need to tie it around you. Then she's going to pull us up. Let me know when you have it and you're ready, okay?"

Tosha had a good grip on the root, and it was comforting to be next to the dirt wall, and not just dangling out in the middle like Patty was. She didn't know how Patty was managing to stay calm and work with the rope, but she found that confidence reassuring. When Patty lowered the last part of the rope down towards her, it was out of Tosha's reach. "I can't reach it. It's too far away from me," Tosha shakily called up to her cousin.

Patty quickly swung the rope back and forth in the direction she had seen the ladder fall in. "I'll get it to you, just grab it tightly when you see it."

Tosha extended her arm, feeling around in the blackness as far as she could. Finally, she managed to connect with the rope, and attempted to tie it around her. She quickly realized, however, that it was impossible to both hold the root and work the rope around her waist. She felt panicky. How on earth was Patty able to do it, she thought. "Patty, I can't do it! I can't hold onto the root and tie the rope around me. How did you do it?" Tosha cried out in a tone of exasperation.

Patty was terribly worried about her cousin, but still felt amazingly calm. Then she had an idea. "Tosha, everything will be all right. I'll have Emma lower me down to you so I can help. Don't worry, okay! Just hold on!"

After what seemed like an eternity, Emma reappeared only a few feet above Patty. She called down, "Tosha, Patty, I'm here! Are you both all right?"

Patty quickly shouted up to Emma, "The ladder collapsed and Tosha fell down a long way. She was able to grab hold of a root and is hanging on, but she can't manage to tie the rope around herself. You need to lower me down to her so I can help her get it tied around her waist. Do you have enough rope on your end to lower me down that far?"

"Oh dear," Emma replied with deep concern in her voice. "I think I do. Oh, please hold on tight and don't move. I have to pull the rope that's tied to you off of the post, and slip it over the mule's hauling-harness, the less movement on your end of the rope the better." Patty was about to tell Tosha that Emma was back and to pass what she had said along to her cousin, when she heard Tosha call out, "Okay," from below. Patty took a deep breath of air and held it. She didn't want to make Emma's task any more difficult than it already was. Silently, she prayed that Tosha would have the strength she needed to hold onto the rope that was keeping her from falling into the darkness.

Several feet below her, Tosha was silently saying her own prayers. She slowly pulled in a big breath of air, closed her eyes and waited for Patty to come help her. Everything seemed to become deathly quiet. Then she heard something very close to her, but couldn't imagine what it might be? She knew Patty couldn't possibly have gotten down to her that fast. Her eyes popped open. In the blackness, she looked around searching for whatever it was she had heard. From the depths of the dirt wall just above her, she thought she could see a root, but it seemed to be moving. What! She thought, that's impossible, I must be hallucinating. Slowly she squeezed her eyes to slits, no longer comfortable with them being completely closed. She kept them glued to the suspicious root.

Emma pulled the mule over to the post. She looked at the rope and placed her hand on it to test the tension. She was very nervous about this, if she wasn't strong enough to hold the rope while she slid it over the harness, tragedy would follow. Emma took a minute to think. If she failed and Tosha fell to the bottom of the tomb, she could never live with herself. She could go for help, but was afraid Tosha wouldn't be able to hold on that long. Realizing there was no time to waste, she looked over and noticed another rope strapped to the mule. Suddenly, her face lit up, she knew exactly what to do. She pulled the extra rope off the mule and tied it through the loop that was over the post. Holding the rope in her hand, she hurried over to the mule and made two loops over part of the hauling-harness and then pulled it tight. She secured it, then ran back over to the hole and called down.

"Patty, I did it! Now we definitely have enough rope to reach Tosha. Hold on really tight while I pull the rope off the top of the post. There will be a jolt, so please prepare yourself for it." Emma dashed back over to the post, and while coaxing the mule to back up she stood next to the post with both hands on the tight rope. As the mule backed up, Emma waited for the loop to be pulled away from the back side of the post. It only took a few seconds for this to happen, and the instant it did she pulled up on it, snapping the rope off of the post. Now, Patty's fate was totally dependent on the strength and ability of Emma and the mule. Emma called down to Patty, "It's done. Are you ready for me to lower you down to Tosha?"

Patty had felt the jerk on the rope that Emma had warned her about, but it hadn't been nearly as bad as she had thought it would be. Hearing Emma's words, she prepared herself. "Yes, I'm ready," Patty said. She tightened her grip on the rope. She had slipped the glowing marble into the pocket of her shorts minutes earlier. She knew she would need both hands and every ounce of strength she had to handle the job that awaited her. She felt herself descending deeper into the hole. She called down to Tosha, "Emma is lowering me down. Do you see me yet?"

Tosha looked up above her, grateful for the distraction from the disturbing root. But, because she was over to the side, she couldn't see anything straight above her other than more dirt. "No, I can't see anything, I'm too far over. All I can see is a dim light coming down the tunnel from the torch at the top, but I can tell you're closer because I can hear you better."

Poor Tosha, Patty thought. She's way down deep in this dark place all by herself. Patty felt good about doing this brave thing for her cousin. It had always seemed like Tosha was the one helping *her*, now she could return the favor. As Emma continued to lower her, Patty searched the darkness for her cousin. She was soon rewarded by Tosha's shriek, "Patty, I see your feet, you're right next to me, I can see you!"

Patty looked up and called out to Emma, "I've reached Tosha, just lower me down a little more, and then stop." Patty ducked her head down so she could see her cousin. As she did this, she reached in her pocket for her flashlight. She switched it on and was overjoyed when she got her first glimpse of Tosha. Tosha's face was covered with dirt and smudges. Patty was surprised to see how dirty she was, definitely not the squeaky clean Tosha she was used to seeing. Nevertheless, she was positively overjoyed at seeing her and wanted to hug her for about a year but she couldn't, not yet. She had to keep her cool until they were both safely on solid ground. Patty checked out the situation with her flashlight. Tosha was only a short distance away from her, but Patty realized she would have to swing herself over in order to actually reach her. She eyed another root that was located just above the one Tosha was clinging to. Her plan was to grab hold of it with one hand, and helping Tosha with her free hand they would work together to get the rope tied around her cousin. It was not going to be easy, but Patty was confident that they could do it. Again, Patty called up to Emma, "I can't quite reach her, she's over to the side. I'm going to swing myself on the rope until I can get to her, okay?"

Hearing this made Emma very nervous. She tried to imagine what Patty and Tosha were dealing with. She felt so guilty, this was really all her fault. She kept questioning herself, wondering if there was something else she could do. She wanted to go for help, but she couldn't possibly leave them all alone. She felt so useless. Tears stung her eyes and she worked to blink them back. Leaning over the opening she listened for any calls from below. She needed to stay alert in case they needed her help.

It didn't take much for Patty to get the rope swinging. She had slipped her flashlight back in her pocket because she needed both hands free. There was very little light filtering down from above. Now she was close enough to reach up for the root she wanted to grab onto. She hoped it would be strong enough to hold her but she was disappointed to feel it slip loose from the dirt wall as she swung away from her cousin.

When that happened, everything seemed to fall apart, both her plan of rescuing Tosha and her courage. Shockingly she heard Tosha scream out in pure terror. Dangling there on the rope, a worried Patty looked over toward her cousin trying to figure out what had caused her to scream. She was afraid that Tosha had lost her grip and had slipped down further. Patty's eyes darted over and she was relieved to see that Tosha was still next to the dirt wall in the same spot she had been earlier. Even in the darkness however, she could see her cousin's terrified face as she swung back to her. "Tosha, what's wrong?" Patty yelled out, desperate for an explanation.

"Patty….let go, let go of it!" Tosha screamed at the top of her lungs, while pointing back at her cousin.

Suddenly Patty felt something moving up her arm. Trembling, she forced her eyes to move over to her right hand and terror gripped her by the throat. There was a snake wrapping itself around her arm, and to her horror, she was still holding it in her hand, her fingers wrapped around it. Screams ripped from her and echoed through the tunnel and out the opening, almost knocking Emma to the ground. Patty instantly understood what

Tosha was trying to tell her. She was terrified as she jerked her arm up and down with such fury that the snake flew through the air like it had acquired wings.

Neither girl knew where it had gone, but they were relieved that it was no longer on Patty. For a brief moment, Patty thought how fortunate it was for her that she had a rope tied around her waist, because otherwise, she would be at the bottom of the tunnel. Shaking from the trauma, Patty worked to calm her herself down, her whole body was trembling. She felt her grip tighten on the rope that suddenly, she was very tired of holding onto.

"Patty, are you okay…please talk to me!" Tosha cried out softly to her cousin. "It's gone, Patty, it's gone."

Emma called down wanting to know what was happening. "Patty, what happened? Are you all right?"

Tosha was the one who responded this time. "It's okay Emma. We had a problem but everything is okay now." Watching her cousin, she saw Patty shake her head back and forth. "Patty there is a good strong root right here next to mine. Get close enough to me so I can grab you, then I can help you get a hold of it. Let's try it that way."

Patty started the rope swinging again. Keeping her eyes on Tosha she grumbled, more to herself than to her cousin…"I can't believe I was holding onto a snake, I hate snakes." Swinging back and forth once again, she moved closer. As soon as Patty got close enough, Tosha reached out and grabbed her, then quickly moved her hand over to the root. Patty held onto it tightly as she used her free hand to pull up the other end of the rope. Together, Tosha and Patty worked in the darkness to maneuver the rope into a knot around Tosha's waist. Both girls exhaled, releasing the breath they didn't even realize they had been holding. "Okay Tosha, are you ready to get out of here? I know I sure am!"

Tosha nodded her head up and down. "Me too Patty, me too!"

Patty yelled up to Emma that they were ready to be pulled out. First it was Patty that felt the even, gentle pull of the mule hauling her up. Then she could feel the added tension on the rope that was around her waist as Tosha let go of her spot on the wall of the tunnel. She gently swung out and both girls swayed back and forth as they were being pulled to the surface.

Patty was the first one Emma grasped and pulled out of the hole. Both of their faces showed a fair amount of dirt, just as Tosha's had. Patty stood beside Emma and stared down into the tunnel anxiously waiting for her cousin to come into view. The mule continued backing up slowly and within minutes, Patty and Emma squealed with joy as they saw Tosha's grimy face looking up at them. They held onto Tosha until she was well away from the hole. Patty grabbed her cousin with both arms and gave her the biggest hug of her life. Emma stood back just a little and watched them. When they looked over at her, she started apologizing. Emma went on and on about how it was all her fault, and that she was so grateful that no one got hurt, or worse. Suddenly, Patty and Tosha scooped Emma into their arms and all three laughed and cried while holding on to one another.

Finally, they stepped apart and Emma helped the other two get untied. All three then fell to the ground and took turns hugging and talking and crying. Once they got everything out of their systems, they composed themselves. Patty and Tosha both reassured Emma that it wasn't anyone's fault. "Emma," Tosha said, "you couldn't possibly have known that there was going to be an earthquake, or whatever it was that happened down there. We wanted to go into the dig just as much as you did."

"Yeah," Patty added, "and even though it was the most terrifyingly stupid thing I've ever done, it turned out okay so don't blame yourself. It was an unbelievable adventure, the kind you only read about in books." Patty presented her brightest smile, even though she really didn't feel like smiling. She was glad to see that it made Emma feel better. They all brushed off what dirt and grime they could and tried to shake off the memory of their near tragedy.

The three girls were all very relieved that it was over. Emma picked up the two ropes and ran over to the mule, removing the other end of the rope from him. Working with the ropes, she wound them back into neat loops, then she attached hers back onto her belt and the other one to the mules hauling-harness. Excusing herself, she asked the girls to wait where they were while she returned the mule and tied him up with the others.

Patty and Tosha watched her walk the mule over to the area where they had seen a number of mules earlier, before their risky adventure began. When she was finished, she turned and started walking back toward them. Then, suddenly, she stopped. She was standing near one of the torches, and the girls noticed a tall gentleman walk up to her. It didn't take long for Tosha and Patty to realize that it was Emma's father. They could hear his masculine voice.

"Emma," her father almost shouted. "What on earth are you doing out here at this hour, and why are you dressed in your dig gear? No! You've been down in my dig, haven't you?" He was clearly angry with her.

She tried to explain, "But father, I have to..." Emma attempted a protest, but her father put his hand firmly on her shoulder and steered her back in the direction of the city.

His deep voice was very stern as Patty heard him order his daughter to return with him to the hotel immediately. He didn't see the two young girls standing in the shadows near the entrance of the dig, nor did he notice Emma glancing over her shoulder back toward them, her face covered with more apologies.

The cousins' hearts sank as they saw Emma retreat with her father. She was looking back over her shoulder at her new friends, wishing she could have said good bye to them. The cousins watched until Emma and her father were completely out of sight, their shoulders slumped with disappointment. "Well, I guess we're on our own," Patty said, feeling total exhaustion flood her body. Looking over at Tosha, she asked, "What do we do now?"

# CHAPTER ELEVEN

# THE JUNGLE

"Let's find the trunk and go home. We can't be too far from it. The marketplace is right over there, and the camp isn't far beyond that," Tosha said, pointing in the direction of the outdoor market. "Can you remember exactly where we were when you jumped out of the trunk?"

Patty looked over at the narrow row of tables lining the street. Everything looks so different at night with no people around. "I'm... I'm not sure," she responded. "I jumped out so fast and ran after Chatters, I don't remember. Nothing looks the same. Maybe if we just start walking around, we'll recognize something."

"That's a good idea," Tosha replied. "Come on, let's go." Tosha and Patty started walking and within a few minutes, they were in the middle of the Marketplace. Patty was surprised to see that there was merchandise left out on the tables, mostly cages with white cloths draped over them. Briefly, she wondered what might be in those cages. Her mind wandered back to all the different kinds of animals she saw in cages during their first visit to the marketplace.

As they walked farther into the market, it got darker, and they realized there weren't any torch lights in this part of the marketplace. Both girls had forgotten to grab their backpacks during their frantic escape from the child emperor's bed chamber and out of the dig. Tosha whispered to her cousin, "I sure wish I had my backpack. I would love a flashlight right about now." Tosha had forgotten that Patty had used hers in the tunnel when she was lowered down to her.

"Oh, Tosha, I have mine. It's in my pocket." Patty reached into her pocket, grasped her flashlight and pulled it out. As she pulled it from her pocket, however, the marble from the tomb fell out onto the ground and rolled a short distance behind her. A soft glow spread out all around them. Patty's eyes grew large as she looked down at it. She backed up and reached down for the marble, but in doing so, she accidentally bumped into a vendors table. A series of loud bangs and crashes followed and Patty knew she had accidentally knocked something over. She straightened up and looked behind her. There were a number of cages lying on the ground.

Tosha heard all the ruckus behind her and looked around just in time to see a dark shadow run across the street, just behind Patty. Tosha screamed. She ran over, and grabbing her cousin by the hand. She started pulling her down the street in the opposite direction of the ominous figure. "Patty, we need to get out of here, *right now!*"

"But Tosha," Patty protested. "I dropped the marble, I need to go back for it."

"Patty, I don't think so. I saw someone back there. We can't go back, I think we're being followed."

"What do you mean, you saw someone. Who? Maybe it's Emma and she's come back to help us."

"No," Tosha said, "it definitely was not Emma." Tosha's voice was tense. Without further questions, Patty followed her cousin down the dark street, still holding the flashlight in her hand.

What had Tosha seen, and why would anyone be following them? Just the thought of it made the hair on the back of Patty's neck stand up, and she felt a cold chill travel down her spine.

Both girls felt panic closing in on them. Tosha could hardly see where they were going, but she felt that using the flashlight would be a mistake right now. They needed to put some distance between them and whoever it was she had seen in the street behind Patty.

Moving along at a fast pace the two girls crashed into and tripped over something big and then tumbled to the ground. Before Tosha could get to her feet she heard Patty shriek. Patty grabbed a hold of her cousin. "Tosha, Tosha," Patty cried in a high-pitched voice. "Look, we found it! We found the trunk, our trunk! Can you believe it?" Patty was simply ecstatic.

"Sh-h-h," Tosha scolded her cousin in a low voice. She asked Patty for the flashlight. Patty immediately handed it to her. Tosha held the flashlight in front of her, but then she paused. Cautiously, she looked over her shoulder to see if anyone was behind them. She didn't see anyone, so she quickly switched it on just long enough to see what they had fallen over. Relief flooded through her as a smile replaced the frown that had been covering her face. Patty was right, it was their traveling trunk. She turned the flashlight off and without further delay Tosha reached for the lid. Patty helped her open it and they both climbed in, pulling the lid down as they lowered themselves. Patty wedged her fingers in the top corner of the trunk in an effort to hold it closed while Tosha worked her magic with the diary.

Tosha turned the flashlight back on and reached for the diary with trembling fingers. She started quickly flipping through the pages. Tosha felt like she was coming unglued, she knew Patty was counting on her, but she was unsure of what she was looking for. She couldn't reveal her doubts to Patty, she just had to figure it out. Tosha's mind was racing as she moved through the pages. She came across some blank pages and stopped suddenly. She didn't remember seeing any blank pages looking through the diary before. Then something really creepy happened. As she stared at the blank pages, words started appearing. Letter by letter the page was being covered in the same bold script as all the other pages she had read from. Even more shocking was what was being written.

*The two cousins were entering the deepest part of the jungle. They were about to encounter their greatest adventure of all time.*

Tosha's hands were now shaking so hard that she could barely read the words as they appeared on the page. She wanted to close her eyes and slam the book shut. This was NOT supposed to be happening.

Patty kept urging Tosha to hurry, keeping her voice as low as possible. She was afraid that whoever or whatever followed them would find the trunk and them inside it. She feared she could not hold it shut well enough to protect them from an invasion. She strained her ears listening for any sounds outside the trunk. Patty's curiosity was beginning to get the better of her, she wanted to know if someone had followed them. Was there someone out there at this very moment, searching for them? Patty glanced over at Tosha who seemed completely engrossed with her nose in the diary. Patty decided she would raise the trunk lid just enough to take a little peek. She felt certain that if someone was out there, they wouldn't notice the lid opening just a tiny crack.

Slowly and silently, she raised the lid just enough to see out. At first she didn't see anything, so with enormous relief, she started to slowly lower the lid. Suddenly, she caught a glimpse of a dark figure moving in the shadows, then it just stood there in the semi-darkness. Her entire body stiffened. At first she wanted to scream, but instead she bit down hard on her lip. She couldn't give away their hiding place. Peering through the crack, she strained her eyes trying to get a better look at the stranger. Silently she released her clenched lip. She was amazed as she realized exactly what it was she was looking at. It was a chimpanzee, just a few feet away from the trunk. He must have escaped from one of the cages when they knocked over the table at the marketplace. She wondered if he realized they were inside it. Patty was relieved that it was only an over-grown monkey that had been following them. He didn't seem nearly as menacing as if it had been a man shadowing them.

Still, curious as to what the hopefully friendly chimpanzee was up to, she watched through the crack and was surprised when she saw him move to a sitting position and seemed to be looking right at her. Patty actually got the impression that he was laughing at her. His small, shiny eyes had a definite hint of humor in them. Patty wanted to smack him for scaring them so badly. She felt a little silly about being frightened. Quietly, she lowered the lid and sat down inside the trunk. She glanced over at Tosha once again, pondering whether or not she should tell her cousin about the false alarm. She decided not to, she didn't want to interrupt her just now. Patty sat very quietly thinking about the chimpanzee. Little did she know that her cousin was desperately trying to figure out how she was going to get the trunk to take them home.

Bump! Bump! From outside the trunk they felt several hard bumps, one of which nearly pushed the trunk over with its force. This was followed by loud screeching sounds. Patty knew it was time to tell Tosha about the chimp she had discovered, and show him who was boss. Patty and Tosha looked at each other. Tosha pulled herself away from the mysterious diary page. She wondered if the man who was following them had found them. She instantly sat up tall inside the trunk and in a low voice, whispered to Patty, "Oh dear, I think he found us!"

"Yes," said Patty, matter-of-factly. "In fact I'm sure he has, and I'm going to take care of him right now." This was Patty's chance to get even with that pesky chimpanzee that had frightened them so much. She pushed the lid of the trunk open and stood up. She had total confidence that she could handle the situation.

Tosha was shocked at Patty's aggressive attitude. It wasn't in Patty's nature to take charge, certainly not in scary situations and Tosha felt this was a very dangerous mess they were in.

Tosha was sure her cousin must have lost her mind, but before she could protest, the lid was fully opened. Tosha stood up next to Patty. The brightness outside took them both by surprise. They slowly blinked their eyes until they adjusted to the bright sunlight. Once they could see, Patty's confidence began to evaporate. Where were they? What had happened to the chimpanzee and the marketplace? Huge plants were all around them. They found themselves looking up at the biggest trees they had ever seen in their lives. Tosha looked over at her cousin in disbelief. "What happened?" Tosha asked Patty in amazement.

"You're asking me?" Patty shrugged her shoulders and held her hands out with palms up. "I have no idea. You're the one working the magic with the diary. I assumed we were still in the marketplace in the dark! I was just sure all the banging we heard was done by that awful chimpanzee. He was sitting right there in front of the trunk, just staring at me. Oops," Patty said as she covered her mouth with her hand, glancing over at her cousin. Too late, the words had been spoken aloud.

"Patty, what are you talking about?" Tosha asked with a frown. "What chimpanzee? What's going on?"

"While you were reading the diary, I peeked out of the trunk to see who might be following us, and I saw him. I didn't want to bother you while you were working on getting us home, but forget about the stupid chimpanzee right now. How did we get HERE? What were you reading in the diary?"

"Nothing," said Tosha. "I was just flipping through blank pages, puzzled because I didn't remember any blank pages from before, and then out of thin air words started appearing on the blank page, like magic. The diary was writing about us, while I watched. Patty, did you hear me?"

"Tosha, did you do this on purpose? I thought we both wanted to go home? Haven't we had enough adventure for one day?"

"I have nothing to do with this, it's the trunk and diary, honest. I thought I could get us home, I really did, but the truth is I have no idea how to get us out of this mess. There, I said it. Now you know. I have *no* idea how the diary and trunk work. They just seem to do whatever they want to do. Now here we are deep in some jungle, who-knows-where, with trees taller than most buildings." Tosha threw her hands up in the air and pointed at the trees that surrounded them.

"Oh Tosha, tell me you're kidding! You don't mean it." Patty looked at her cousin, searching her eyes for the truth. As she looked into them she was troubled by the answer she saw. Patty dropped her arms to her sides and her shoulders slumped. "Now what are we going to do? We might never get home! Tosha, I would never have gotten back in this trunk again if I had known you couldn't get us back home. What are we going to do?"

"Patty, I don't know. All I can tell you is that so far the trunk has taken care of us. Even though we've been scared out of our wits, everything seems to work out okay in the end. We get into one mess, only to fall into another. I believe the trunk and diary will take care of everything, I really do! Remember, we left the trunk at the edge of that camp? How is it that we tripped over it in the marketplace, right when we needed it most? And guess what I found in the bottom of the trunk under the diary... both of our backpacks! How strange is that?"

"Oh wow, no way! This is all so weird!" Patty said, shaking her head back and forth. "Why do you think it's doing all this to us?" Patty questioned her cousin.

"I don't know, I still don't understand why, or how, this is happening. It's like the trunk is on some adventure kick, and it wants us to come along. Then, Tosha climbed out of the trunk and she handed Patty her backpack. Patty eagerly grabbed the backpack and hugged it to her.

Tosha started looking all around them, trying to think of what their next step should be to address this newest turn of events. "I do remember reading a few of the words the diary wrote, and it did write something about a jungle."

Reluctantly, Patty followed her cousin's lead and climbed out of the trunk. They started walking on a barely-visible pathway. "What are we going to do?" Patty asked with a worried look on her face. She just wanted to go home.

"Well, for starters, I guess we better look around and try to find a road or something," Tosha replied. They were now some distance from the trunk. Tosha was thinking about whether or not they should turn back and go in a different direction since she couldn't see any sign of civilization, when.... BANG! BOOM! Large round coconuts came slamming down from above and crashed to the ground right next to her.

"Run, Patty, run for cover!" Tosha screamed as she darted from the path of another oncoming coconut. Tosha ran hard and fast to escape the heavy assault from above. Patty followed right behind her, dodging back and forth. She looked back over her shoulder trying to figure out why the raining coconuts seemed to be following them. High in the trees she saw several monkeys bouncing from tree to tree, knocking loose leaves and small branches.....and coconuts. The monkeys were curiously chasing after the girls from their treetop hideaways.

Their escape would have been a lot faster if it weren't for the tall plants. After a few minutes, the two cousins found themselves following what appeared to be a skinny path in the massive undergrowth of the jungle. Neither had a clue as to where they were going. It felt like they had been running hard for a long time when suddenly the path ended and they found themselves in a clearing. Patty fell to the ground, out of breath and holding her side.

"Tosha…let's rest for just a little bit…okay. This seems like a safe enough place." Patty squeezed the words out of her aching lungs. Tosha was already collapsing on the ground next to her cousin. She was just as eager for a break as Patty.

"Okay, this looks good to me too," Tosha panted.

While they caught their breath, Patty asked her cousin to explain to her exactly what she had witnessed the diary doing.

"Patty, I told you. I opened it, searching for the last page we had read, and came across some blank pages. I was looking down at one of them, thinking I hadn't seen any blank pages before, when words started appearing. Written words, one-by-one, and you are not going to believe this, but it was writing about us being in a jungle."

Patty's mouth dropped open. "How could that happen? Maybe you imagined it. After all, we were both scared out of our minds."

"I know. I can't explain it, but I'm telling you exactly what I saw," Tosha said, shaking her head back and forth. "Why don't you tell me about the chimpanzee you saw, and I'll let you know if I believe *your* story?"

"Very funny! You saw it too, you just couldn't tell what it was." Patty then explained the entire chimpanzee story to Tosha. "I just wanted to see if someone was out there, and then when he looked like he was laughing at me, it made me mad!"

A big smile spread across Tosha's face as she pictured a pesky chimpanzee teasing her cousin. "Well," Tosha said grinning, "it does seem like all little furry things have a strange attraction to you." Tosha worked very hard to suppress the giggles that tried to escape her lips. She was sure it was a tense moment for Patty, but to hear Patty tell the story, it sounded pretty funny."

"Okay smiley," Patty said to her cousin. "While we're confessing things, why don't you tell me how you think we got here? Why did you make me believe that you had the trunk and diary all figured out?"

"I didn't say anything to you earlier," Tosha explained, "because I was sure I could figure everything out. I just thought I needed more time. That's why I took the diary home with us, but it vanished out of my backpack. I never had the chance to read it or try to figure anything out. I did have a theory. I thought the trunk would take us to whatever page I read from, but now the diary has some blank pages and appears to be writing us into its history! I wasn't reading anything when it brought us here. I was just watching the words as the diary wrote them, but I'm positive that the diary is magic, and so is the trunk. It's as if they can't be separated." Tosha paused and took a deep breath. "Patty, like I said before, I still think the trunk and diary will take care of us."

Patty was on the ground facing Tosha. She was on her side and propped up on one elbow, listening to every word her cousin said. When Tosha was finished, Patty sat up. She looked at her cousin with disbelief. "You think everything is going to be okay? Tosha, look at us. We don't have any idea where we are except that we are in the middle of a jungle, and the trunk is back there somewhere, maybe even smashed by coconuts. Are we supposed to just sit here and wait until the trunk decides to come find us and take us home?"

Tosha had to admit it sounded impossible, but in her mind it was the only explanation for the strange events that had occurred. Besides, she liked the idea of the trunk and diary being magic, she was ready to accept the unexplainable. Patty just needed more convincing. She was about to offer her cousin more evidence when she heard Patty let out a startled gasp. Tosha's head turned to see her cousin staring toward a thick group of trees at the edge of the clearing. Patty hovered close to the ground, her hand stretched out in front of her. Without speaking a word, she pointed a trembling finger at something she saw in the trees.

Tosha strained her eyes, searching the thick jungle. Not seeing anything of interest on the ground, her eyes traveled up, and there it was. Perched high up in the trees was a house. "Oh my gosh, it's a tree house!" Tosha squealed. "Can you believe it?" She was so excited about Patty's discovery. She wondered what it would be like to live way up there. "Wow, this is so cool! Do you think anyone lives in it?" Tosha asked, full of curiosity. She had already picked her backpack up off the ground and was starting towards the tree house.

"Tosha, Tosha, come back here," Patty hissed in a low voice. Thinking quickly, she reached out and grabbed her cousin's ankle, almost causing her to fall. Patty thought the rickety house looked completely unsafe. It had long vines growing all over it and they swayed in the breeze like a bad haircut. She could see holes in it, and the entire house was leaning to one side.

"What are you doing Patty? Let go of me. Don't you want to check it out?" Tosha couldn't understand why her cousin was still on the ground. What was she waiting for?

Patty slowly stood up. She looked at her cousin, and then glanced toward the trees. Tosha, I'm beginning to think that the brain fairy missed you when she was handing out good sense. So did the fear fairy for that matter...are you nuts? I'm not climbing way up there. You said yourself that you wondered if anyone lived in it, are you really prepared to meet the natives? They could even be cannibals. Do you want to be the main course for their dinner tonight?"

"Oh Patty, you don't really think that." Tosha couldn't pull her eyes from the tree house. Patty moved over and was standing next to her cousin. Both girls stood at the edge of the clearing, gazing towards the tree house in the dense jungle. All sorts of exotic sounds filled the air as birds and various creatures went about their daily activities.

"Tosha, I really think..." Patty was about to suggest that they go back and search for the path that would hopefully lead them to the trunk, but her sentence was cut short by the overwhelming feeling that something was very wrong. Her voice froze. Silence fell over the area. The girls no longer heard the birds and other jungle sounds. Patty felt that all too familiar chill running down her back. She reached her hand over and grabbed her cousin's arm. "Tosha," she whispered, "something or someone is watching us. Can you feel it?" Patty's eyes then caught a glimpse of something very large moving in the dense jungle.

Tosha agreed with her cousin, something was eerily wrong. "Do you see it? Where is it?" Tosha asked Patty in a low whisper. Patty could not form the words. She felt as if her whole body had turned to stone. She couldn't even get her arm to move so she could point at it. Instead, she slowly rolled her eyes over to the right, in the direction of the movement.

When her cousin didn't respond, Tosha turned her head and looked at her. Seeing the frightened expression on her face, Tosha looked at the same spot that Patty was staring at. Tosha searched the edge of the jungle, her eyes trying hard to catch sight of whatever might be hiding in the shadows of the trees. She had a creepy feeling about it too.

"Patty," Tosha whispered, "I really think this would be an excellent time to check out that tree house you didn't want to explore. I'm going to count to three, then we'll both run for it, okay? Just run for the tree house, keep running and don't look back." Tosha had no idea what was out there watching them, but she was really hoping that it couldn't climb trees. Fear gripped her so hard she was having trouble breathing. Forcing herself to calm down, she started counting, keeping her voice as low as possible, "One...two...THREE." Grabbing Patty by the hand she ran straight for the tree house. Neither one looked back, they just ran as hard and fast as they could.

The tree house was, thankfully, not too far from the clearing where they had been resting. Both girls were frantically looking for an entrance as they covered the distance between them and the tree house. There had to be stairs, a ladder.... something! Tosha was the first to spot it. On the far side of the enormous tree was a long, rough-looking, vine-like rope that had been made into a ladder. Briefly, Tosha remembered the last ladder she had been on and wondered if this was a good idea, but quickly put her fears out of her mind. This was their only chance of escape for now.

Patty knew that whatever had been lurking in the jungle was now chasing them. She could hear it running through the grass, she thought she could even hear it breathing. It seemed very close and very big. The ground shook as it ran after them. Patty tried not to think about the angry sounds she heard behind her. She knew if she looked back, it would all be over and she would not be able to go on. Trying to close her mind to the sounds and the fear, Patty remembered the last words Tosha said to her; keep running and don't look back!

With a rush, the two cousins pushed their way through bushes and tall grass. The tree house was right there, only a few feet away now. Tosha pulled Patty in the direction of the rope ladder, not allowing her to slow down. Tosha urged, "Come on Patty. Don't let up, we're almost there!" Tosha heard the same sounds that Patty heard. She already had her hand stretched out, ready to grab the make-shift ladder. Together, both girls jumped onto it and immediately started climbing as fast as they could.

Reaching what she thought was a safe distance, Patty's curiosity got the better of her. She had to know what it was that had chased them to this massive tree and farther away from the trunk, farther away from home. She looked up to see her cousin ahead of her, still climbing. Patty paused, squeezed her eyes shut and took a deep breath as if doing so would give her the courage she needed. Slowly, with only one eye barely open, she looked over her shoulder and down toward the ground. She could make out something very large moving towards the tree they were climbing. It was dark gray and almost bounced through the tall vegetation that covered the ground.

Patty froze on the ladder as a loud, trumpeting noise filled her ears. She opened both eyes wide and, in horror, stared down at the gray thing thundering towards her. She could not take her eyes off of the creature. Above her, she heard Tosha screaming, "Patty, come on, get up here. Hurry....Hurry!" Her cousin's voice snapped her out of her trance, and she again turned all her attention to climbing the ladder to safety. The ladder went through a hole in the floor of the tree house. Once she was through the hole, she jumped off the ladder and joined her cousin. The two girls grabbed each other and tumbled to the floor.

"Sh-h-h-h," Patty said, "let's keep out of sight and stay really quiet. Maybe it will give up and go away."

"Patty," Tosha whispered, "don't you think we should try to pull up the ladder? What if it climbs up here?"

Patty frowned as she said, "No way. I got a pretty good look at it, and whatever it is, it's definitely too big to climb that ladder."

"Wow, you saw it? How big is it? What did it look...?" Tosha stopped in mid- sentence as the air filled with the loud angry sounds of the beast below. It made both girls jump. They covered their ears with their hands. The sound was so loud it actually hurt their ears. "Patty," Tosha's stressed voice whispered, "are you absolutely sure it can't climb the ladder?"

"Yes, I'm sure," Patty said confidently. "It's so big I could feel the ground shake as it ran after us, couldn't you?"

"Yes," Tosha said reluctantly. "I felt it too, but you saw it. What is it?"

"All I could see from the ladder was a giant gray blur. It moved through the jungle like an enormous bowling ball. It was awful. I just want to go home," Patty said, sounding discouraged. "How are we going to get back to the trunk now? We'll never be able to find the path we took to the clearing!"

The jungle grew calm and a variety of birds sang and flew about. A gentle breeze moved through the tall trees and Tosha could feel the tree house sway back and forth. Lying on the floor, she observed her surroundings. The roof had several holes in it, though most of them were very small. There were four openings that Tosha guessed were windows. They were just square holes in the wall, and there was one on each of the four walls that surrounded them. They had no screens or glass in them, the tree house appeared to be abandoned. She noticed twigs and leaves scattered all over the floor. Then Tosha saw something. She jumped to her feet and ran to the other side.

Patty didn't even notice. She had her eyes shut, with her arms crossed over her face. She was tired, thirsty, hungry, and dirty. She listened for any signs that the beast was still nearby. Thankfully, the soft sounds of the jungle felt much friendlier now than they had earlier. She actually found herself relaxing. She hated to admit it, but she did feel safer here than she thought she would. She pulled in a deep breath and slowly exhaled. Suddenly she heard Tosha gasp. Patty's eyes flew open and she sat up. "Tosha, what are you doing? You're making too much noise," she whispered.

Patty was sure the noise her cousin was making would draw attention to them. Wearing a concerned frown, Patty watched her cousin approach an opening that looked like a window, and lean out of it. "What on earth are you doing? If you fall, I'm not coming to rescue you this time," Patty said with more confidence than she felt. She knew that if her cousin actually got into trouble again she would help her any way she could. A couple minutes later, Tosha pulled herself back inside, and when she turned around her arms were loaded with bananas and other fruits. Patty was overjoyed, she pulled herself up onto her knees and stretched out her arms wiggling her fingers. "Oh, Tosha you are my hero! I can't believe it, you found us something to eat! I am starving!"

Tosha walked over to Patty wearing a giant smile. She sat down next to her cousin and both girls dug into the fruit as if it were Thanksgiving dinner. Eating away, Tosha glanced over at Patty as she peeled her third banana. Smiling brightly Tosha said, "You're welcome."

Patty's big brown eyes looked back at her, "Oh yeah, thank you, thank you! I was so hungry. I'm sorry, I guess I get a little grouchy when I'm hungry."

"Ya think," Tosha replied. "It's okay." Looking around her she said, "You know, this place isn't so bad, for a home away from home."

"Well," Patty said, "I hope you don't plan on moving in, because I *do* want to go home, and I definitely don't want to be here at nighttime. This place would really be spooky at night."

"I know what you mean, I don't want to be here at night either," Tosha agreed. Changing the subject, she said, "That sure hit the spot, now if we could just find something to drink. I'm really thirsty. The fruit helped, but it can't take the place of a nice cold glass of water."

"You've got that right," Patty said. They sat there for a while enjoying the jungle noises and the gentle breeze blowing through the tree house, and then decided to stretch out. Patty felt her eyes getting heavy. Within minutes, they both fell asleep.

Bump, bump, bump...the sound brought the cousins to an upright position. Having been startled out of a much needed nap, they found themselves confused and disoriented. They looked at each other's sleepy faces.

"What was that?" Patty asked, wearing a worried frown on her face. "Where are we?" Patty took in her surroundings quickly. Before Tosha could answer, she said "Oh, never mind, I remember now. We're in the middle of a jungle nightmare!" With that, she laid back on the floor and closed her eyes.

Tosha stood up and started looking around to see if she could figure out what was causing the annoying bumping sound.

The noise didn't bother Patty nearly as much as it did Tosha. She liked to wake up slowly, unlike her cousin who always hit the floor running. She had decided it was a light sound so it couldn't possibly be the giant gray thing, and that was all that mattered to her. Patty allowed herself a renewing stretch and a small yawn. Her eyes were thin slits as she laid there for a few minutes. Suddenly, she thought she saw something on the roof. She opened her eyes all the way and focused on one of the holes above her. Then she saw it again, a black blur shot across the hole, then another, and another. Patty giggled and called out to her cousin. "Oh Tosha, I think we have company."

Tosha was several feet away. She spun around and came over to where Patty was lying on the floor. She looked down at her wearing a questioning frown on her face. "What are you talking about?" she asked.

Patty couldn't stop giggling as she stood up and pointed toward the ceiling. Tosha's eyes followed. "That's where the noise is coming from. There's a bunch of monkeys up there, and they're chasing each other around. They've been following us since we left the trunk. They are responsible for the flying coconuts that were bombarding us earlier. I saw them jumping around in the trees as we were running to get away."

Tosha's eyes roamed across the ceiling as she saw them jump over one hole and then another. "Well, you must have invited them, because monkeys seem to really like you," Tosha said, wearing a big smile. As her cousin's giggles became contagious, both girls laughed and pointed, and then laughed some more.

Suddenly, Patty let out a squeal. She pointed to the largest hole and elbowed her cousin. When Tosha looked over, she couldn't believe her eyes. One of the little monkeys was poking his head down through the hole and looking at them. "He must have heard us talking," Patty said. While the girls laughed at the monkeys' antics, the mischievous little things took turns peeking down through the holes at the girls. It was as if they knew it made them happy. The girls fell to the floor and were nearly doubled over from all their laughing. Finally, the little guys left and the cousin's continued to lay there for a while, catching their breath. It was a wonderful break.

Tosha briefly wondered what time it was as she looked at her watch for the hundredth time. Not one minute had ticked by since that morning when they had walked into the attic and climbed inside the trunk.

"Gosh, I'm thirsty," Patty said. "Maybe we should look around this place and see what we can find. Do you think anyone lives here anymore?" Patty questioned, looking around the room.

"I was wondering the same thing, but it sure doesn't look like it to me. Let's check it out and see what we can find," Tosha said with her usual curiosity.

The room they were in was fairly large for any room, much less a treehouse. It seemed to be the only room in the house. It was constructed mostly of skinny poles and long brown grasses. The treehouse was more round than square, having four windows placed in such a way that the occupant had a full view of the jungle below.

The girls worked their way watchfully around the room, each going in the opposite direction, examining different things they found. When they came across anything interesting, they called the other over and examined the item together. Tosha was on one side of the room and Patty on the other.

"Patty," Tosha called suddenly. "Look at this! It looks like there is another room here."

Patty looked over and saw Tosha looking up toward the ceiling. She was pointing at a square hole, much like the one in the floor where the rope ladder was.

"Wow," Tosha sighed, "there must be another room above this one. I wonder how we can get up there."

Across the room where Patty was standing, she had just noticed a ladder propped up against the wall. "Would this be good enough to get us up there?" Patty replied, lifting it off the wall. Tosha ran over to help her with the tall ladder, and together the two girls struggled to put it into place. Once they were satisfied that it was secure, they gathered up their backpacks. Adjusting them onto their shoulders, they prepared for the climb.

Tosha looked at Patty and said, "You go first and I'll follow right behind, okay?" She was worried that Patty might stay behind and not join her in exploring the upper level, but felt strongly that it was important they stay together.

"Okay," Patty said as she worked to swallow the lump that had developed in her throat. She felt her courage disappearing as quickly as her curiosity. She found her thoughts flashing back to last year when her grandpa had been cleaning out the gutters of his house and fell off the ladder, breaking both of his arms. What if something like that happened to one of them? She didn't think Grandma would magically appear to rush them to a hospital, even if one existed in this jungle. Patty took a deep breath and pulled her shoulders back. She could do this, it was no big deal really. She closed her eyes and reluctantly started up the ladder.

"Patty," Tosha said. "I really don't think you should climb up there with your eyes shut. What are you afraid of, anyway? There isn't anything to worry about."

Patty opened her eyes just a little and frowned down at her cousin. "What makes you so sure? Remember what happened to Grandpa last year?"

"Patty, Grandpa didn't have Grandma standing at the bottom of the ladder, holding it steady for him. I am right here, and I'm holding it for you. I'm not going to let go until you're completely off of it, and safe. When you get up there, you can hold it for me from the top, okay? Now come on, keep moving," Tosha encouraged, reaching her hand up to gently push her cousin along.

"Okay, okay, I'm going! Don't get pushy!" Patty worked her way up the ladder. As she moved up and climbed through the hole in the roof, she could see the jungle far below her. As she continued to climb, she thought to herself, this would be much easier if these were stairs instead of this narrow passage

built of bamboo. She climbed some distance before she came to
a second hole. She passed through it and stepped off the ladder
with a sigh of relief. She did as her cousin instructed and held the
ladder from the top until Tosha joined her.

Patty's mouth fell open as she looked around. When
Tosha stepped off the ladder, a gasp escaped her throat too.
"What an awesome view," breathed Patty. This was not a room
at all, but a lookout tower. It was about the size of a closet, with
a short railing built all around the edge. There was just enough
room for the two of them, and the tower was just above most of
the trees. The view they had was the most beautiful sight either
girl had ever seen.

"Oh look, Tosha, over there at the edge of those trees, is
that a waterfall?" Patty asked excitedly. Tosha was afraid Patty
might fall out of the tower in all her excitement.

"It sure looks like it," Tosha replied. "Do you suppose
that water would be safe to drink?"

Patty turned to look at her cousin. "I don't care. I'm so
thirsty I would drink anything at this point, even my mom's icky
coffee. I'm going to go over there and drink until I can't hold
another drop." Patty was not going to take no for an answer.

"All right," Tosha responded. "I suppose *any* water is
better than no water at all. Let's go." The girls turned toward
the ladder and Tosha headed down first. Grasping the ladder,
she stretched her leg out to climb on. Suddenly she froze, her
eyes open wide with terror. She stared intently at the ladder
below her. Slowly climbing up it, was the biggest snake Tosha
had ever seen. Nearly in shock, her breath came in short, hard
gulps.

Patty was in a big hurry. She had never been so thirsty
in her life. Impatiently, she waited for her cousin to go down
the ladder, all her thoughts focused on the cool wet water that
splashed down the waterfall a short distance away. She wasn't
used to not having her daily needs met. She decided she would

never again take the little necessities of life for granted. "Tosha, what is the problem? If you want me to go first, I'd be glad to."

Tosha heard every word her cousin said, but still did not speak. She simply did not know what to do. She wanted to scream, but that might scare Patty right off the tower. The snake was one of those really big ones. Tosha had seen them before at the pet shop. A boy at school had bragged about having one for a pet. Her mind raced as she weighed her options. Cautiously, Tosha forced her leg to slowly move as she backed away from the ladder.

The minute Tosha started moving away from the ladder, Patty assumed that her cousin wanted her to go first, as she had just suggested. Without hesitation, Patty moved into Tosha's spot and jumped onto the ladder, eager to get moving.

Tosha's mouth flew open and her words rushed out. "Patty Jo, get off that ladder right now! There is a snake the size of the Empire State Building on it, right under where you're standing."

Patty did not question her cousin, but took immediate action. She pitched herself back off the ladder so fast that the two girls collided. Tosha lost her balance and fell backward against the railing, pulling her cousin with her. Out of control, both girls frantically grabbed for anything that might keep them from falling out of the tower.

A sick feeling filled Patty as she felt herself falling over the railing. Tosha managed to grab one of the straps on Patty's backpack. The sound of their screams mixed with loud cracking noises filled the air as the railing broke with the unexpected weight of the two girls. All thoughts of the snake, of their persistent thirst, of the trunk, of everything left their minds... everything except the need to hold on. Patty felt her hand grab part of the broken railing as she went over. Holding on for dear life, she screamed out to her cousin who was clinging tightly to the backpack strap, "Hold on Tosha, don't let go!"

"I won't! I won't!" cried Tosha.

The jungle was full of large vines woven up and down through the trees. One of these vines was within inches of Tosha's grasp. "Patty," Tosha yelled, "there is a vine right here by me. I'm going to grab it!" She reached out for the vine. As she held it tightly with her right hand, she loosened the grip of her left hand from the strap on Patty's backpack. "Hold on Patty," pleaded Tosha. With another quick move, Tosha completely let go of her cousin's backpack and wrapped both her hands tightly around the vine. Tosha called out to Patty to do the same. She could see the railing barely holding together. She knew it was only a matter of seconds before it broke away from the tower completely. Looking just above Patty, she saw that her cousin should be able to reach the same vine. "Patty, reach out with your right hand and grab the vine, its right above you!"

Patty was frightened, but she cautiously looked to her right. Without hesitating, she grabbed the vine just as the railing broke away completely from the tower and dropped to the jungle floor. Patty had never been so scared in all her life. She found herself wishing she were back at Graybrook. The mansion didn't seem bad at all compared to the mess they were in right now. "What's next, Tosha, we can't hold on like this for very long!"

"Let's work our way down the vine," Tosha replied in a shaky voice. "Just don't look down. I think I'd faint if I saw how high we really are."

Together, the girls began to slowly inch their way down the vine. They had only traveled about five feet, when the vine started pulling loose from somewhere up above. Terrified, the girls stopped their descent and held their breath, gripping the vine with all the strength they had left. At first it slipped only a little, then more and more. The next thing they knew, they were gliding through the air, just like Tarzan. As they swung through the jungle the vine continued to slip, lowering them down to the ground as they glided along. Within seconds, the girls went from screaming to giggling with delight.

This is more fun than any roller coaster at an amusement park, Tosha thought as the jungle air rushed across her face. It took less than a minute for them to hit the ground. The girls went rolling across the grass as they landed. Out of breath and still laughing hard, they both laid there for a while. "That was so much fun. I can't believe we did that without breaking our necks!" Tosha said breathlessly.

Patty shook her head back and forth and replied, "I can't either." Both girls had big smiles on their faces.

# Chapter Twelve

# THE WATERING HOLE

Looking up into the trees they could see the broken tower, now only rubble. Tosha caught sight of two red parrots sitting on a limb just to the right of the tree house. "Look Patty, those parrots are watching us. They probably wish they could swing on a vine like we did. I'll bet it looked really cool from up there!"

Patty sat up and looked over at the parrots. Smiling she called to her cousin, "Tosha that was the most..." Her sentence was cut short as Tosha pointed toward the parrots again. "Patty, the parrots aren't looking at us. They're looking at something right behind us."

Terror struck their hearts as they heard the dreaded sound from earlier that day. Patty's head turned in the direction of the ear piercing sound. The ground shook as the large gray beast came rushing through the jungle toward them. Patty had seen enough. Eyes wide open and full of fear, she got to her feet and started running. Tosha was right behind her cousin, she had gotten a good enough look at it to recognize what it was.

"Patty," Tosha screamed above the noise. "It's an elephant...a wild elephant!" Running as hard as they could, with no real direction in mind, they plunged their way through the thick jungle. Eventually the sound of the elephant seemed to be more and more in the distance. Now a new sound filled the air. This sound was straight ahead of them. It was a steady, roaring noise, and was getting louder with every stride they took. The air had taken on a new feeling as well. The cool wet freshness that hit the girls' faces almost felt like rain, so much so that their hair was getting wet.

Tired and thirsty, Patty didn't know how much further she could go, when suddenly the jungle floor disappeared beneath her feet and *splash…splash…*both Patty and Tosha fell several feet into a large pool of water below them. Patty felt her feet hit the bottom and then pushed off toward the surface. Bobbing up and down she opened her mouth and gasped for breath. She blinked her eyes and glanced over at the bank where they had fallen in. She was surprised to see the drop off was only about six feet, she expected it to be much farther. It was an awful feeling to just fall off like that. With her heart pounding in her chest she treaded water while calling out for her cousin. "Tosha, where are you?" Patty screamed out as loud as her exhausted voice would allow.

"Here I am. I'm right behind you." Tosha swam over to her cousin.

Patty didn't know whether to laugh or cry. In a high panting voice she said, "Thank goodness we weren't on a forty foot cliff. I don't even like jumping off the diving board at the pool! And look, we found the waterfall. Isn't it beautiful?" Patty's finger pointed in the direction of the colorful waterfall. Brilliant gigantic flowers surrounded the entire area, as well as a large number of parrots and other exotic birds. The vision was like a post card, too beautiful to be real.

They swam over to the falls and didn't hesitate capturing the cold water in their hands and drinking. After their thirst was completely satisfied they thought they would rest on some big flat rocks located near the water's edge. When Patty turned to swim over to them she saw something move out of the corner of her eye. She slammed her eyes shut. She was afraid to look, fearing it was the pesky elephant that had chased them there.

The sound of the waterfall had served to temporarily drown out any noise he may have been making. Now both girls froze as they heard a huge splash. Neither had seen anything come up to the edge of the pool. Nevertheless, they both knew that the elephant that had been following them was now in the water with them. "What is it with this thing, what have we done to make him chase us like this?" Patty screamed, her voice on the edge of total panic.

They were both very good swimmers and were now rushing toward the rocks they had spotted earlier. Tosha was the first to reach them, and Patty was right behind her. Once they reached the rocks they quickly climbed them to safety. Slowly they turned to search the water for signs of the intruder. Sure enough, standing in the shallow part of the water was a baby elephant. It stood only knee deep in the pool, and was sort of rocking back and forth, shaking its head, looking right at them.

"Oh my goodness," Patty exclaimed. "It's only a baby. Is this little guy the same noisy, scary thing that's been bothering us all day?"

As if on cue, the baby elephant threw back his head, and let out a mighty blast.

"Yea, I'd say that's him alright," Tosha said, covering her ears with her hands.

"He's too little to make so much noise," and with that remark Patty covered her ears as well.

Tosha screamed above the roar. "Amber is little too, but she makes more noise than anyone else in our house," Tosha said smiling. She didn't want to admit it, but she actually missed her baby sister. The little elephant walked deeper into the water toward the girls. Standing on the rocks, watching him come closer, Tosha started backing up.

"Oh Tosha, he's just a baby. He won't hurt us." *Splash…*

Tosha was shocked to see her cousin jump in the water without fear. With her mouth hanging open she stood there and watched Patty swim the rest of the distance to the elephant. The first thing she did was climb on his back. To Tosha's amazement, this didn't bother him at all. In fact he seemed to enjoy it.

"Come on Tosha, get in, he just wants to play. I think he's lonely." Patty giggled as she reached out and rubbed him on the top of his head. He bobbed his head back and forth and then filled his trunk with water. He then proceeded to squirt the water out his trunk and gave Patty the shower she had been longing for. He seemed harmless enough. Carefully, Tosha joined her cousin, ready to enjoy the cool water and the baby elephant.

The three of them played and splashed and drank more water. Then Tosha spotted an area by the waterfall where the rocks made a natural water slide along the edge of the falls. This was far too inviting to pass up. They played, swam and sunned themselves for the rest of the afternoon.

Finally, they climbed out of the pool. "I think we should name him," Patty suggested with an affectionate smile on her face. "How about Thunder, because that's what it sounds like when he makes that awful noise." Patty loved animals, and they all seemed to love her, all except snakes that is.

"Yea, I guess that would be a good name for him," Tosha said, sounding a little distracted. "Patty, I think it's time to get out of here and find the trunk. Let's see if Thunder will give us a ride. We'll make great time with him doing the walking."

Grabbing their backpacks and climbing atop Thunder, Patty said, "I wonder if he's lost, or if he even has a mother? Maybe something happened to her, and he doesn't have anyone to take care of him."

"Well, I don't think you should get too attached to Thunder. We have to go home, and there's no way he's coming with us. Your mom wouldn't even let you keep Chatters, so she definitely wouldn't let you keep an elephant, even if he is a baby. Besides, your mom would never believe we found *him* in your neighborhood," Tosha said, laughing at her own joke.

Patty rolled her eyes. "Don't be silly Tosha. The trunk is big, but it's not that big. He would never fit. Besides, I would much rather have Chatters as a pet. I really miss him, don't you?"

Tosha tilted her head to one side and said, "No, not really. He was really cute, but I prefer my cat."

Tosha guided Thunder in the vague direction she thought they needed to go. They were bobbing up and down, happy to not be fighting the thick jungle's underbrush. The elephant carried them along, but suddenly Thunder stopped. He stuck his trunk high in the air sniffing loudly. He seemed to be alarmed. Tilting his head back, he let out one of his famous ear-piercing cries. The girls immediately covered their ears with their hands. Something was terribly wrong, but what? Thunder started rocking back and forth, back and forth.

"Tosha, I have that bad feeling again, something is wrong with him. What do you think…" Before she could finish her thoughts the baby elephant took off running as fast as his short legs would carry him, all the while sending his loud cries out through the jungle. They had no choice but to hold on tight. Within minutes they heard another elephant somewhere in the distance returning Thunder's cries.

Just as quickly as he started running, he stopped. Both girls flew off head first and found themselves laying face down in the thick vegetation. Shaking their heads, they slowly stood up and looked around them. "Oh no, we're back at the tree house again. I don't believe it," Patty said sounding frustrated. She glanced over at Thunder and he was rocking back and forth again. "Well, I don't think we're going to get anymore free rides from him. Which way do you think we should go from here? If we can just find that trail again it should lead us back to the trunk," Patty said brushing off her shorts.

"A-a-a…I don't want to alarm you Patty, but I think we better get back in the tree house. I have a feeling Thunder has found his mommy." Tosha's voice grew more and more intense as she spoke.

Patty looked in the direction of Tosha's gaze and saw a very, very big elephant headed right for them. "Let's get out of here, *now*!!" Patty screamed. She and Tosha ran for the rope ladder of the tree house. Up they climbed. This time Patty did not stop to look back, she just kept on climbing. Once they were in the tree house, they breathed a sigh of relief. They were safe and sound, or so they thought. *Crack, cr-r-r-ack,* the whole tree shook and trembled. They were knocked off their feet. Falling to the floor, they looked at each other in shock.

"I think mommy elephant is mad. She's trying to knock us out of this tree house," Tosha said in disbelief as she tried standing. Once again, she was knocked to the floor. This time the fall sent her rolling across the room and she slammed into something hard. She looked up and cried out in amazement, "Patty, Patty, look, it's the trunk. Quick, let's jump in!" Tosha stood up, supporting herself by holding onto the trunk.

Patty tried three times to stand up, and every time the tree house shook and cracked under the angry attack of the mother elephant. Patty decided to crawl across the floor to where Tosha stood. This worked very well, and within seconds Tosha was helping her to stand. Tosha held on tight to Patty and together they lifted the lid of the big trunk. Leaning over they fell inside and the lid slammed shut behind them.

The two cousins lay back, too exhausted and too frightened to think of anything except home. Neither one said a word. Tosha snatched up the diary, and was holding it tightly against her chest. Being back in the trunk again, they both felt safer. It was a welcome feeling. In the semi darkness the girls tried to relax. *Wham...wham!* The trunk was being pushed and shoved back and forth as the tree house continued to shake violently. They desperately held onto each other inside the shaking trunk. Back and forth they went.

Frantic, with her eyes full of hope, Patty turned to Tosha. "Can't you get us back to the attic the same way you did before?"

Tosha looked at her cousin thoughtfully. "That's it, that's it!" Digging in her backpack she found her flashlight. She switched it on and opened the diary. This was no easy task with the constant jolts from below. Tosha dropped the flashlight twice and the diary once. Patty took the flashlight from her cousin's shaking hands and shined it onto the pages of the diary as Tosha searched for the page she needed. At last, there is was...

*This was a day of great adventure for the two cousins. They went back to the house and this time they both went inside. The big old house was scary, but they were determined to explore it.*

The banging and trembling continued until suddenly they felt the trunk tipping over. Tosha dropped the diary and they reached for each other....SMASH!! Holding on tightly, they felt themselves roll out of the trunk as it crashed over on its side. She was terrified that the whole tree house was about to come crashing down, with them still in it. Desperately clinging to each other with their eyes shut, they held very still. Patty was unwilling to move or to open her eyes. She feared they had rolled out of the trunk and were dangling over the edge of the branches, and she couldn't bear to see such a terrifying image. Tosha was equally as frightened as her cousin. Still clinging to each other they could hear themselves breathing hard. In fact, that was all Tosha could hear. With her face squinted, she slowly allowed one eye to peek out at their surroundings.

"Wow!" Tosha sighed allowing a big smile to cover her face. "We made it back, we're in the attic. The trunk *is* magic, I told you so!" She let go of her cousin and slowly sat up.

The instant Patty heard Tosha's words her eyes flew open. She didn't move right away, instead she looked around the room they were in. She was so happy...so relieved. She just wanted to savor the moment. It was like being lost at sea for weeks and then finally being back on solid ground. It was an incredible feeling.

Tosha was standing up. Patty pulled herself up and stood beside her cousin. Her legs felt shaky, and it seemed that her entire body still swayed back and forth. On trembling legs Patty walked over to the trunk and placed a big kiss on the lid. "Thank you, thank you very much for getting us back home. I'm sorry I ever doubted your magic." Turning around she said, "You were right Tosha, you said all along that the trunk and diary would take care of us, and they did."

Tosha wore the brightest smile she ever had. "Yeah, it worked," she said, letting out a sigh of relief. "All I had to do was read about being in the mansion, and *poof,* here we are."

# CHAPTER THIRTEEN

# THEIR RETURN

Wasting no time they ran for the stairs, both eager to head for home. On the way back they talked about the exciting day they had had, and the magic of the trunk and diary. It had been a fantastic journey. So much had happened, and yet here at home no time had passed. According to Tosha's watch they had been gone just a short time.

"Patty, wouldn't it be awesome if Emma lived right here in your neighborhood," she said thoughtfully. "We could see her anytime we wanted to, and the three of us could explore all kinds of stuff. I loved the way she talked, her accent was cool. I've never heard anyone that sounded the way she did. I already miss her."

"So do I," Patty agreed. "I'm glad Chatters belongs to her. Since I can't have him for my own, at least I know someone like Emma is taking good care of him. I sure hope her father wasn't too angry with her. It wasn't her fault, Emma would never have gone into the dig if we hadn't been there to go with her. I still can't get over all the crazy things we did. I feel like I just stepped out of a history book, don't you?"

"Yeah, sort of," Tosha replied. "I have always wanted to do something totally out of control like that, to go someplace different and exotic. It was like a dream, a dream come true. I want to tell someone about it, but we're going to have to keep this adventure to ourselves. Can you do that Patty?"

"It will be hard, but we have to. Besides, no one would believe us, I can't even believe it," Patty said looking at her cousin. Her big brown eyes sparkled.

When the girls arrived home, Patty's mom was happy to see that they did not have the noisy little animal with them. While Patty and Tosha had been gone taking care of the monkey problem, she had talked to Patty's father about Chatters. They both gave the pet monkey idea a lot of thought, and the two of them decided they would consider it. She knew her daughter was very fond of Chatters. Having an animal like that in the house was a big responsibility, and it would have been up to her daughter to take care of him. Her mother had to admit, she was relieved that the girls had found his rightful owner. Maybe they could see about getting her a puppy this summer. "So," her mother said, "it looks like you girls found his owner? It sure didn't take you very long."

Patty didn't see her mother standing in the kitchen when they came in the house. She jumped and spun around, searching for the right words. "Oh yeah…well, we sure did. It was easy, he jumped right out of my arms and ran straight to his…his… owner." Patty stammered as she twisted her hands together. The mention of Chatters brought back all sorts of bitter sweet memories for Patty. She couldn't help but miss him even more. She hung her head and started to walk back to her bedroom, Tosha was right on her heals.

"Oh wait Tosha," Patty's mother added, "I almost forgot. Your mom called and she's on her way home. She was able to finish her business early, and she will be picking you up first thing in morning. You need to be sure you have all your stuff together and packed, okay?"

"But she said I could stay all week. Do I have to go home?" Tosha couldn't believe that her visit was cut short. Of all the trips her mom had gone on, she hardly ever finished up early. Why this one?

Patty's mom was surprised by her question. "Well honey, you can stay as long as you want to. I'm just telling you what your mother told me over the phone this morning. You girls can set up another over night any time you want." She watched as the two girls walked down the hall, they were obviously upset. She figured it had to be because they missed the frisky little monkey.

The girls were so disappointed. They hung their heads and walked to Patty's room. "Gosh," Tosha said, "I thought I'd get to stay at least five days. It may be weeks before we can get together again." In the back of her mind she wondered if Patty would ever want to travel in the trunk again. She had to admit she wasn't even ready to answer that question herself, so she decided not to bring it up.

Tosha and Patty took advantage of their last day together. They spent most of the day talking about the adventure they had that day. Now that they were safely home, the entire thing seemed unreal.

When bedtime came, they were exhausted. For them it had been a very long day indeed. They both climbed up onto the top bunk together, Patty at one end and her cousin at the other. Patty lay on her back, staring up at the ceiling. "You know Tosha, I think you're right about the trunk, I mean about how it took care of us and kept us safe. I'll bet that no matter where it took us, we would always get back home safe and sound. Do you think the diary recorded our jungle adventure? If it did, I'd sure like to read it just to see if it sounds as neat as it was."

"Yeah, I'm sure it did. I saw it putting the word jungle on the blank page…that was so weird." Tosha shivered. "And what about our evening with Emma? That would really be awesome to read about. I was so terrified I don't actually remember much of it. You seemed so calm, how did you do it?"

"Well," Patty said, remembering the amazing marble. "I'll tell you, it's weird, but I swear that marble I found in the tomb had something to do with it. I can't explain it. It was as if just looking at the marble gave me everything I needed and wanted. I was hanging on for dear life, and I so badly wanted to be strong. You know, to figure out what to do, and how to do it. I wanted us to get out of there without dying. The whole situation seemed hopeless. But when I looked into the marble all my fears and doubts disappeared. It was like I suddenly knew what I needed to do, and I did it without fear."

"Gosh, do you think it had some sort of magical powers too?" Tosha asked with a small frown creasing her forehead.

"I think so. I sure wish I wouldn't have dropped it. Oh Tosha," Patty sighed, "we have to go back just one more time. I want to read the diary, and I want to see Emma, don't you?" Patty looked down toward the foot of the bed at her cousin.

Tosha sat straight up in bed. "You do, you'll go back again?" She couldn't believe Patty was already talking about another adventure in the trunk. They couldn't make any definite plans right now, but they both promised each other the next time Tosha spent the night they would go back to Graybrook one more time. With this on their minds, they pulled the covers up and snuggled in for a good night's sleep.

# CHAPTER FOURTEEN

# THE WOMEN'S LEAGUE

Tosha's mother came to pick her up first thing that morning. On the drive home Tosha was unusually quiet. Noticing this, her mother became concerned. "Tosha, what's on your mind? You're never quiet, don't you feel well?"

"I'm okay I just wasn't ready to leave Patty's yet. You said you were going to be gone for a week." As soon as the words were out of her mouth, she knew she was in trouble. She hadn't intended it to sound so bad.

"Well, I missed you too," her mother replied, sounding a little disappointed in her daughter's attitude. "I thought you'd be glad to see me, and see what came in the mail while we were gone. It's from the Women's League."

Tosha immediately brightened. Her mother had her full attention. "What...what did you find out mom? What does it say?" Tosha asked eagerly.

Her mother handed her a fat envelope. Glancing at it Tosha could see it hadn't even been opened yet. "I didn't open it yet. I thought we could look it over together."

Tosha gave her mom a big smile. "Really, can we do it as soon as we get home?" She was already opening the envelope. She hoped it would answer some of the many questions about the Wareham family. The drive home was a short one, and Tosha had just started looking at the contents of the envelope when they pulled into the driveway.

"Let's get your things inside and then we'll sit down at the kitchen table and go over everything they sent. I'll see if Dad will entertain Amber for us," her mother said. A few minutes later Tosha and her mother sat at the table. With the pages all spread out in front of them, they started reading. Each time one of them found something of interest, they read it aloud to the other.

"Oh Tosha, here's something you'll want to hear. It says that the Wareham family had only one child, a daughter born June 1919. Her name was Emily, and her mother died shortly after giving birth to her. After that, her father started traveling a lot. He was a famous archeologist."

Tosha dropped her pages and looked over at her mom. Even before her mom read the words archeologist, she knew. Emma was Emily. The beautiful girl who shared her clothes with two total strangers was the same girl that her mother was reading about, and was the same girl who grew up at Graybrook and had her tiny feet prints stamped into the cement patio. All this time Tosha wanted to know more about the family who built the mansion, and without realizing it, she had traveled in the trunk and had dinner with them just yesterday.

Her mother was still reading, "She is now living in a retirement complex in the area."

The last words her mother read shook her thoughts back to the present. "What, what did you say mom? Would you read that last part again, please?"

"It says that Emily married after her father's death, and she moved away from Graybrook. A few years ago her husband passed away. It says here that six months ago she moved back and is living in a retirement complex near the mansion."

Tosha was visibly shaken, but tried to act calm. "Does it say where the complex is?"

"No, but I'm sure we could find out. We could call the Women's League and see if they have her address."

"Mom, how old would Emma be now?"

"Emma. Who's Emma?" Her mother looked at her with confusion in her eyes.

"Oh, did I say Emma…I mean Emily…yeah…that's what I meant to say…Emily. How old would she be now?"

With a thoughtful frown on her face, Tosha's mother looked back down at the paper she was reading. "Well, let's see. She was born in 1919, and it's 1999 now. That would make her eighty years old."

"It's so hard to believe that she lives close by. Why doesn't she live at Graybrook anymore?" Tosha was full of questions, but so unsure of which ones she could ask without slipping up and making her mother suspicious.

"It says here that her father was injured and could no longer work. After she married she moved to Europe and locked the house up. By the time she returned the house was too much for her to take care of. She's donating it to the Women's League. Honey I have to start getting lunch on the table. Why don't you take all this and keep it in your room. We'll look at it more later on, okay?" Her mother got up and started working in the kitchen.

Tosha took everything to her room. Spreading all the pages out on her bed, she searched for the one her mother had been reading from. Once she found it she read it over and over again. She didn't know how she would manage it, but she had to get Emma's address. She had to see her, talk to her. Tosha couldn't imagine the elegant little girl being eighty years old. Holding the paper in her hand she let it slip out of her fingers as she lay back on her pillows, thinking of Emma.

She needed to talk to Patty. Together they would find Emma. Tosha wanted to call her cousin, but that was impossible. She would have to choose her words too carefully in case her mother overheard their conversation. It couldn't be done over the phone. She would have to wait until they could talk face to face, but how long would she have to wait?

Tosha didn't notice the additional information on the back of the paper she had been reading. There were a number of photographs highlighting some of the items from the mansion that were in storage. The Women's League planned on placing some of these items in the mansion once they took possession of it and turned it into a museum. The photo at the bottom of the paper was a painting of Mrs. Wareham from 1914. She was wearing a beautiful braded chain around her neck, with a teardrop charm dangling from it. The young woman was beautiful.

Later that week Tosha was thrilled when her mom announced that the family was having a get together the following weekend. They had planned a cookout and everyone was going to be there, including Patty's family. She could hardly wait to tell her cousin the news.

The cookout was at Grandma and Grandpa's house. Tosha and her family were in the car and on their way. Once they arrived, Tosha was excited to see that Patty was already there. Jumping out of the car she found her cousin and told her there was something very important she needed to talk to her about. They moved away from the group, and walked down by the lake to talk in private.

"Patty, you're not going to believe what has happened," Tosha said almost bursting with enthusiasm. "Emma…Emma… she's back. I mean she lives in your neighborhood. She's eighty years old and is right here in town." This was not coming out the way Tosha had wanted it to. She was too excited and she wasn't making any sense.

Patty frowned at her cousin. "What are you talking about? What do you mean Emma lives around here?" Patty thought her cousin had traveled one too many times in the trunk, it must have affected her mind somehow. Looking at Tosha with a mixture of sympathy and confusion in her eyes she said, "Tosha, that's impossible. Where did you get such an idea?"

Her cousin tried again, this time she chose her words more carefully. "Okay, when my mom picked me up last week from your house, she had received news from the Women's League. There was a whole packet of information about the family. Mr. Wareham, the one who built Graybrook, was an archeologist and had a daughter named Emily who traveled with him all over the world." Tosha expected a big reaction to this incredible news, and when she didn't get it, she tried again. "Patty, don't you get it? Emily is Emma! Our Emma, and she is eighty years old!" Tosha watched as Patty's eyes grew enormous with the impact of her words.

"Did you see her, where does she live? How can you be so sure it's our Emma? There were probably lots of girls named Emma or Emily back then," Patty said, wondering if this could be possible.

"No, I haven't seen her, not yet. But Patty, I'm right about this. The letter even said that Emily's mother died not long after she was born, just like Emma told us. Look!" Tosha dug into her pocket for the pages. She had brought some of the information with her. When she pulled them out a couple of them fell on the ground. Patty bent over and picked them up. She unfolded them and that's when Tosha noticed the items pictured on the back of one of the pages. "I didn't see this," Tosha said, eagerly snatching the page out of Patty's hand. Both cousins sat down in the grass and examined it together.

Suddenly Patty let out a squeal and jumped to her knees, pointing to the photo at the bottom of the page. "Look Tosha, isn't that the necklace that Emma was wearing when we went to dinner with her? The one you liked so much?"

Tosha jumped to her feet. Bouncing up and down she said, "Yes, yes it is! This proves it, it all fits. It's got to be her, I want to go see her, and no I don't have her address yet. But I do have a couple ideas on how I can get it. My mom is going to ask the Women's League if they could give us Emma's address. In the meantime, I plan on doing some research of my own, just in case they don't have the address. I'm going to call every retirement complex in the area and ask if there is anyone by the name of Emma living there. I'm not sure what her last name is now. The papers said she was married shortly after her father died, but it didn't mention her husband's name."

Patty was so excited. "Tosha, this is amazing. This means the trunk belonged to Emma. I wonder if she ever traveled in it like we did. That's one of the questions I'd love to ask her. Call me as soon as you find out, okay?"

The next week Tosha was on the phone a lot. She called every complex that was listed. Not a single one had an eighty year old renter by the name of Emma. Five days after the cookout, her mother came home from work with good news. "Tosha, I have a letter from the Women's League. I put it on your bed for you."

Tosha ran to her room and tore the letter open. Inside was at least part of what she had hoped for. The letter said they could not give out address information, but they could tell them the name of the complex, SUMMER OAKS. Tosha got the phone book and looked for that name, but there wasn't one listed. She was getting frustrated.

The next day she called one of the other listings in the phone book and asked if they could help her. "Hello, I'm trying to locate a retirement complex called Summer Oaks. Have you ever heard of it?" To her delight the voice on the other end of the receiver replied. "Yes, it's a brand new complex and is not listed in the phone book yet." They had the address and phone number and gave them to her.

With shaky hands, Tosha dialed the number. After only two rings a woman's voice answered and said, "Welcome to Summer Oaks. How may I help you?"

Tosha jumped when she heard the lady on the other end of the line. It took her a few seconds to find her voice. "Hello...

my name is Tosha, I…I'm looking for a very good friend of mine who lives there. Her name is Emma and I…"

The voice on the other end of the line said. "One moment please, and I'll connect you." Tosha's mouth dropped open. All her phone calls had finally paid off. Oh my gosh, she's there, she's really there, Tosha thought. She was so shaken by this that she panicked and hung up the phone before anyone had a chance to answer. She fell back on her bed and just looked up at the ceiling. Now what should she do? She wanted to see Emma face to face, not just talk to her on the phone. She's so old. She might have a heart attack or something when she finds out that she and Patty are the same kids she met seventy years ago. The next thing she needed to do was talk to Patty. She wanted the two of them to go to Summer Oaks together. This was something they *had* to do together.

The following week Tosha talked to Patty on the phone three times before they finally had both their moms talked into another overnight. It was all set up for the next day, Saturday. Now that the plans were made, every minute dragged as Tosha waited for Saturday morning to come. Impatient, she packed her overnight bag that afternoon. She was very nervous, nervous about what she wanted to say to Emma, and even more nervous about how Emma would react to seeing them. Tomorrow would tell.

Morning came at last. She sat up in bed and enjoyed a nice big yawn. Stretching her arms above her head she looked out her window. She was disappointed when she realized it was dark and gloomy outside. She ran over to her bedroom window and saw the rain drops hitting the patio. She knew this would change her plans, but they had all weekend. Surely it wouldn't rain both days. Once she got to Patty's house, the two girls disappeared to Patty's room and behind closed doors discussed what to do. They would get up first thing Sunday morning and go to church with her cousin's family. Then after lunch they would ask Patty's mom if they could go for a walk around the block. More like five blocks, that's where Summer Oaks was, just a short five blocks away from Patty's house. Then they would find Emma...and then...and then? Tosha couldn't think beyond that point.

Sunday morning they woke up to a beautiful sunny day. They both agreed it was a good sign. When church service was over Patty's family decided to stop at their favorite restaurant for lunch. Sitting at the table, Tosha actually felt like she was going to be sick. She and Patty were not interested in the table conversation, nor were they interest in eating. Their minds were on far more important things.

Finally they were back at Patty's house. The girls changed their clothes and reached for their backpacks. Patty's mom had agreed to let them go on a walk, and they were now on their way. On her way out the door Patty had asked her mom if they could stop by her friends house after their walk, and her mom said it was okay. They just had to be back home by dinner time.

"Tosha, are you sure about this? I mean, what if she doesn't remember us?" Patty was not totally convinced that showing up at Emma's door unannounced was the right way to do this. "I wish we knew what her last name is now, that way we could confirm this Emma is our Emma. What are we going to do if it's not her?" Patty walked along shaking her head back and forth, filled with doubts.

Tosha had not said much all day. She remained quiet, deep in her own thoughts. Patty persisted, "What are we going to say to her?" Patty was talking more to herself than to her cousin. "I know, how about, 'Hi Emma, remember us, we're the two cousins you invited to dinner seventy years ago! And then just for fun we went into your father's dig and nearly died. Remember, your father caught you dressed in all your gear in the middle of the night. By the way, did you get into big trouble for that?'"

Tosha stopped walking and looked over at her cousin. "Patty, don't be silly, this is serious. We don't want to say the wrong thing." Tosha paused, then started walking again. "I don't know what I'm going to say to her. I want to see her first, see if I can recognize her before I say anything." Turning the corner, they looked up to see a big sign. *'Welcome to Summer Oaks'*

Without saying another word, they reached for each other's hand. Walking past the sign they headed for a building marked OFFICE. Once inside, Tosha did the talking. "Hello, can you please help us. We're here to see our friend Emma."

The lady behind the desk was quick to respond. She handed them a small map of the complex and marked the building where Emma lived. Five minutes later, they stood at a door marked 109. "Well, this should be it," Tosha said with no real emotion in her voice. She was numb. She couldn't feel anything at the moment except her heart pounding like thunder in her chest.

Patty was shaking all over as she stood in front of the door. She glanced over at her cousin who seemed frozen. Tosha wasn't moving, she was just staring at the door, waiting. She decided Tosha needed help. Slowly Patty raised her hand and with a trembling finger she pressed the door bell of unit 109.

No sound could be heard as the girls patiently waited. They were beginning to fear that she wasn't home. Tosha's eyes moved to the front window, and Patty was looking down at the door mat. **WELCOME FRIENDS** was stamped on the mat in big fat letters. They didn't hear the footsteps from inside. They didn't even notice the door open, so they were both surprised to look up and see a kind, elderly lady smiling down at them.

Tosha looked first into the eyes of the woman. Then she caught sight of something very familiar. A silver and gold braided chain and dangling from it, the beautiful teardrop with the tiny gold star inside. Patty's eyes locked on the woman's smile. She would know that smile anywhere.

Quietly, the woman bent down and with arms open wide she hugged them both to her and with that beautiful sweet accent she whispered in their ears, "I've been expecting you two. What took you so long?" Tears filled her eyes as she lovingly held Tosha and Patty in her arms.

Tosha felt like she was going to collapse and Patty held Emma even tighter as her entire body started trembling out of control. The girls felt big smiles cover their faces and laughter spilled out with overwhelming emotion. They all three hugged and laughed for a long time.

Emma invited them inside and they spent the whole afternoon visiting. She told them that as a little girl she had also traveled in the trunk. Her father had discovered the trunk and diary long ago in the tomb of a young Egyptian prince. Her father had given it to her as a gift on her sixth birthday. She explained to them that the trunk and diary are magical, but only work for children.

After a long visit the girls reluctantly stood to leave. They knew it was time for them to be heading for home. As they started for the door, Patty stopped and looked back at Emma. "I have one more thing I would like to ask you Emma. What happened to Chatters? I...I...really loved that little guy." Patty's big brown eyes filled with tears.

Emma's eyes softened and she bent down to look into Patty's eyes. "Patty, I've had a variety of pets throughout my lifetime, but none of them were more fun than Chatters. Before you girls leave, I have something for you two. I was just about to get them before you got up to leave. Wait here, I'll be right back."

Patty wiped her eyes and the two girls looked at each other with curiosity showing on their faces. Emma walked down the short hallway and disappeared into a room. Then suddenly, Patty heard a familiar sound. Eeeekkk!! Eeeekk!! Looking up she saw Emma walking towards her with something hidden in her arms.

"Oh, my! It's Chatters!" Big tears filled Patty's eyes as she looked up at Emma. "You still have Chatters? I've missed him so much." Without waiting for Emma's reply, Patty took the furry little monkey and held him close.

Emma smiled down at her. "Well, it's not the same Chatters, but he is related to our old friend. I've been saving him for you, he's yours."

Patty's mouth dropped, as she looked first at Emma and then at Tosha. "I...I..." Patty was at a loss for words, she didn't know what to say. Looking back at Emma, she choked out the words. "What if my mom won't let me keep him? I can't give him up again?

"You don't have to worry, I know your mother will let you keep him. Trust me." Emma had a mischievous twinkle in her eyes, then she winked and smiled down watching the two snuggle.

Patty squealed with delight. Hugging Chatters close to her, she danced all around the room saying over and over, "Thank you...thank you...thank you!"

Tosha laughed out loud as she watched her cousin move around holding Chatters close to her. She was so happy for her. She knew nothing could have made Patty happier than this thoughtful gift, and coming from Emma made it even more special. She watched her cousin playing. A couple minutes later she heard Emma come up behind her. She felt her rest her hands on her shoulders, and then she felt her place something around her neck. Tosha's hand slowly moved up to gently feel the necklace that Emma had placed there. Oh my, she thought. It was Emma's necklace. The one Tosha had admired since the first time she had seen it.

"Emma, you're giving me this...this! But it was your mother's. Don't you want to keep it?" Tosha was shocked that Emma would part with something so special.

Emma bent down and looked into Tosha's eyes. "I want you to have it. This way you will always remember me, and know that we were friends, very special friends."

Tosha threw her arms around Emma's neck and hugged her tightly. She didn't want to ever let go. "I'll never forget you Emma, not ever."


THE END…maybe

CPSIA information can be obtained at www.ICGtesting.com
Printed in the USA
LVOW13s0835250813

349458LV00001B/57/P